BLACK
BOC

KTN,
AK

Vision Quest

KTN
AK

KTN
AK

Vision Quest

a novel

Dan Lundy

Daniel E. Lundy Publishing

Cover photograph by LaRita M. Lundy
Raven photograph © iStockphoto.com/Mr. Sailor

Designed by Meadowlark Publishing Services

Printed in the United States of America
ISBN 978-1-4675-0594-9
Published 2011

Published by Daniel E. Lundy Publishing
PO Box 472
Siletz OR 97380

I dedicate this book to the Siletz Tribal Councils,
past, present, and future,
and to A & D counselors everywhere.
Thank you.

Acknowledgments

First, I thank Creator for giving me abundant life. He has blessed me in more ways than I can express.

I thank my wife, LaRita, for her insightful criticisms and her faithful support in all I endeavor to do. When I was too sick to get out of bed, she encouraged me to finish writing this book.

I thank daughters Bekki, Teresa, and Noni for proofreading the text and giving me wonderful and creative feedback.

To Kelli Albright I will be forever grateful for all the time and effort she put into editing one rough draft after another. Without her skill and encouragement this work would not exist today. She is a friend and a sister.

To my friend and hunting partner Rocky Hoiness, thank you for your help and friendship.

Garris Elkins, who encouraged me, thank you.

I thank Rick Russell for his feedback on the content and his encouragement in "future story possibilities."

Thank you Allen and Linda Palmer for your proofreading and storyline encouragement.

To Sheridan and Stan from Meadowlark Publishing Services, thank you for lending your skill, your expertise, and your personal touch to this story. You are both amazing at what you do.

Thank you to all who prayed for me, my health, and this book. Blessings.

Author's Note

It is important to understand that this story was written from the perspective of a member of the Siletz Tribe who has had the unique experience of living in two worlds and can therefore articulate with some accuracy the polarized views of two cultures:

With few exceptions, the Euro/Anglo culture, the dominant one, considers this land "ours to use" for all the good and healthy purposes necessary to sustain a proper lifestyle for all Americans, as we see fit.

The Native American perspective, for the most part, is that this land is still "occupied" by descendants of conquerors from Europe who appear to be driven to cover the land with concrete and asphalt, use up every possible natural and economic resource, and ignore the spiritual and natural needs of the land and the repercussions of this irresponsible philosophy and its irrevocable results.

Why is "the land" the central focal point? All salient issues filter through the land. All socio-economics are determinants and resultants of the land. We are formed from the land and will return to it. We have the power to affect the land in the short term and the long.

Both of these perspectives are extreme. What I personally believe is this: the Creator has made a way for all cultures to find Him and to honor Him and His Creation and His land, if we will but seek Him.

Preface

The End of an Age

In 1855, after the Battle at Big Bend of the River and after having signed treaties at Table Rock, elements of the Rogue River Indians, the Tututenis (Too-too-ten-ays), the Shasta Costas, and many other tribes were rounded up and force marched to reservations at present-day Siletz and Grande Ronde, Oregon.

Many of the tribal people were beaten by soldiers along the way. Some died of their wounds. Some died from disease (measles, chicken pox, influenza) and others slipped off to fend for themselves, only to starve to death or be hunted down and killed.

Many, especially the very young and very old, died when they were forced to swim the rivers: the

Umpqua, the Coos, the Sixes, the Alsea, and the Siuslaw. Some of the women who gave birth along the way died with their babies; some survived.

The men were bound with ropes around their wrists, then tethered together on longer ropes, forced to move in single file along the trails with armed soldiers at each end of their tethers.

The soldiers, some mounted on horses, others on foot, were carrying rifles with bayonets. Some carried pistols and swords.

Many women and young girls were raped and murdered, their bodies left for the scavengers. A few lived to tell their stories.

Some groups of natives were transported by steamship up the Columbia River and then offloaded and marched to Siletz and Grand Ronde, with short stays at Fort Yamhill and Fort Hoskins.

They were delivered to the reservations at different times, in different ways, and by various routes from many tribes, clans, and places. The Pacific Northwest had been "cleansed" and made ready for settlement by "decent God-fearing folk."

Upon their arrival at the reservations, tribal members were given rotten food and told to build what shelter they could to get through the winter. They were given a choice of religion: either Roman Catholicism or Protestantism. They were "given" a new language, English, and were forbidden to speak the old language. In some cases they were allowed to speak the Chinook Trade language so trade and basic communication could still take place; but the old Rogue River language, Tututeni of the Diina, and other native dialects, were not allowed.

The government did not keep its word in the treatment of the tribes. All the different tribes, even those at war with one another, were thrown together on the reservation. The promised food never materialized. The blankets, the houses, the security vanished in a fog of bureaucratic forgetfulness.

The people's "names" were written onto rolls and changed, as seemed necessary, at the whim of the Indian agent. Very few of the old tribal names were written down and most were therefore lost.

A whipping post was established in order to keep order at Siletz. Stocks and gags were used to keep the peace. Anyone caught practicing tribal dances, songs, storytelling, regalia-making, or the old religious ceremonies in any form was beaten and whipped or stocked and gagged as a public spectacle and lesson to all. A "holding corral" was established as a form of punishment. This allowed tribal members who broke the rules to "walk off" their resentments or insubordinate attitudes publicly.

Order was kept. Tribal people were allowed no citizen rights. They could not vote and could not own firearms, nor could they travel without a pass from the Indian agent. If an Indian didn't return and report in by nightfall, he was considered a renegade and was hunted down and brought back to be punished.

Indians would not be granted citizenship for another seventy-seven years, yet the young men would be allowed to fight and die in the Spanish American War, World War I, and all the wars since.

Per capita, Indian people have shed more blood in wartime than any other race in defending the country called the United States of America. Why? They still consider this land their own.

Different tribes and clans were thrown together as though their individual cultures had never existed. They lived in squalor. Many didn't survive.

Sickness was everywhere. The food that was handed out was moldy, bug-infested, and rotten; most often no food was given at all. Many died from sickness and disease. Many starved to death. Some died from exposure and others from pneumonia. Tuberculosis hit the reservation, killing many. Some died of broken hearts, simply "turning their faces to the wall."

One Siletz man was beaten to death with a revolver for the "crime" of pilfering food. The once proud and self-sufficient people were now relegated to begging for food and dying for the lack thereof.

The one positive thing was that the Siletz River had strong runs of Chinook and Coho salmon, summer and winter steelhead. Eels were abundant and were a staple of the people, as were cutthroat trout and crayfish.

The tribesmen were adept at smoking and drying fish of all kinds. Those who survived the first year put up fish after each run, enabling them to endure in spite of the starvation tactics and broken treaty promises so readily given by the conquest-driven "Americans."

Estimates vary that from 20 to 25 million native people lived upon this land before the Europeans came. By 1885 there remained fewer than 2 million American aboriginals alive. The ethnic cleansing and genocide forced upon this land goes beyond anything seen in modern times anywhere in the world. The killing of 6 million Jewish people during World War II pales in comparison to the holocaust wrought upon the American Indian in the "settling" of America.

America was not settled; it was conquered, sometimes through warfare and at other times by guile and fraud. Most of the original inhabitants were killed, either by war or disease. Their culture was replaced by a more dominant, organized, and ruthless one. The spirit of the people was very nearly destroyed and remains so to this day ... or so it seems.

Vision Quest

1

Talking Circle

It began in a counseling class—actually a Talking Circle. They met in a back office at the Siletz Clinic. The room itself was devoid of character, with bland, white walls, no windows, fluorescent lighting, and gray plastic stackable chairs designed for anything but comfort.

The Talking Circle was an old tribal tradition passed down through the generations as a forum to allow all to speak, all to be heard. It had few rules: Whoever holds the eagle feather has the floor, uninterrupted; everyone is treated with respect; the Circle leader is in charge but promotes equality within the group; Creator is present when the Circle is in session; what is said in the Circle stays in the Circle.

They opened the Circle with prayer to Creator for direction and Smudge, which consisted of burning sage in an abalone shell. The eagle feather and smoking abalone shell were passed in a counterclockwise direction to each person, who used the feather to waft the smoke over their head, heart, and body, thereby asking Creator to cleanse them of evil spirits and bless them. The tradition varied slightly from tribe to tribe but basically followed this general protocol. Sometimes sweet grass or cedar was employed instead of sage. It was, in essence, a visual prayer of cleansing. The chairs were arranged in a circle with a blanket in the center. The abalone shell was put back on the blanket after all participants had smudged, the sage had burnt out, and the smoke had ceased. Other sacred objects were sometimes placed on the blanket, such as tobacco, pieces of tribal regalia, beaded items, and—on rare occasions—a Bible.

Jared Spotted-Horse had never considered the idea of a vision quest. He had heard the old stories from elders who had gone on Vision Quest when they were young, but he knew the old ways had passed on. Besides, the elders—these old guys—they just told stories to pass the time. Who knew if such stories were even true? Sometimes the old full-bloods had some hokey ideas, especially in the age of video games, satellite TV, and the Internet. Vision Quest? Maybe there was a video game called *Vision Quest*. Anyway, the idea just popped into his head like a subliminal message. Maybe Creator planted it. *Sure, Jared*, he thought to himself.

This Talking Circle was more interesting than the other forms of counseling Jared had to endured over the years. The courts had sentenced him to the tribe's alcohol and drug program—A & D—several times. He had listened to his fellow tribal members—men and women, boys and girls, mostly teens—tell their stories of drugs, alcohol, abuse, violence, brokenness. He had heard it all.

Jared didn't really care anymore. He knew he would die just like his Uncle Billy, who had shot himself, or his Auntie Jeannie, the victim of an unsolved murder, or his mom, who died of a broken, alcoholic heart.

Doris Palmer had been victimized since childhood, having been sexually molested by a drunken stepfather. She was removed from the home, only to get passed from one bad situation to the next in the state's foster care system, until she ran away with Jared's father, Tom Spotted-Horse, who introduced her to a life of debauchery and chemical dependence. He had even prostituted her for a year in the Portland area, until one night she was beaten so badly that she almost died.

They moved back to the Siletz Reservation after that. Tom hoped that she would heal quickly so he could put her back to "work." The doctor at the tribal clinic told her that she had to change the way she was living her life. He scheduled psychological counseling for her in the hope that she would deal with some of her "life issues." She didn't keep the appointment.

Tom threatened Doris with divorce if she didn't move back to Portland with him. She refused to go, engaging in one drunken brawl after another with him. He was finally taken to jail one night after he broke her nose. The blood was everywhere when the police showed up and had to pull Tom off and break his stranglehold on her. Paramedics revived her, but she was never able to breathe quite right after that.

She gave birth to Jared a few months later. She was afraid he would come out deformed after the beatings and the drinking, but he seemed fine, born with thick black hair and coal-black eyes. She named him after a cousin who had died of some unknown disease as a child. She told herself, "Let's give the name another chance." So Jared Thomas Spotted-Horse was named.

Jared Spotted-Horse knew in his heart that he would someday be found frozen in a ditch or dead in a car. He might even get into a fight like Jimmy-the-Fox had, getting a knife shoved into his kidney and lying there bleeding to death while the cops stood around and questioned everybody, not even bothering to call the ambulance until everyone was "rounded up." Jared had come by the next day and poured some Budweiser out of a forty-ouncer onto the dried blood in the snow, amazed at how bright pink the blood turned when mixed with fresh powder and beer like that. It seemed to spread out to ten times its original size.

Jimmy's trouble was that he was so damned tough. He had been trained as a boxer in the Golden Gloves program from the time he was a little kid. He knew when to duck, when to weave, and when to step in and throw a hook, a jab, an uppercut, or a cross. He even slipped in an elbow to the throat once in a while. His right cross was to die for, or from, depending on your proximity to Jimmy when he threw it. His fighting name, "Jimmy-the-Fox," was well earned in the ring. His win-loss record was twenty-one wins (eighteen by knockout), one loss, and one draw. The loss was his first fight. The draw was his second. After that he never lost another fight. He learned his lessons well and never repeated his early mistakes. He worked out tirelessly and was in tremendous physical condition. He could run twenty miles and work out for hours. His stamina was nearly without limit.

The night Jimmy died he had stepped outside to settle a dispute over a woman at a party. The two men squared off and began to spar. It was clear that Jimmy was going to win the fight. His antagonist, another tribal member who was a bit less drunk than Jimmy, made a move to swing, then ducked under Jimmy's jabbing punch and tackled him around the waist in a wrestling move and slipped behind him. He pulled a switchblade from his back pocket and drove it into Jimmy's side, twisted the knife, then pulled it sideways toward the spine, opening Jimmy's kidney up and slicing the aorta in the process. He stabbed him twice more in the lungs for good measure. The fight was over before it started as Jimmy slowly buckled to his knees, then collapsed to the ground with one hand on his side in a futile attempt to staunch the blood flow while the other hand grasped at the chest wounds. His eyes were wide with surprise, looking for answers in the blurring faces of the now-silent bystanders who had poured out of the house to witness the fight. He lay on the snow-covered lawn, coughing pink frothy blood, and bled out over a period of ten minutes or so; he quietly awaited death as each breath became shallower and weaker.

Jared's mind drifted a lot during the Talking Circle. The guys and gals were taking turns speaking, stumbling along, telling their stories, and he just couldn't seem to hear them. He saw their lips move, saw the tears running down one fat girl's cheeks and dripping onto a stained Seahawk sweatshirt. Her boyfriend had beaten her, the cops had been called, and the kids had been taken. Jared didn't hear her; he was concentrating on the sweatshirt. *Yeah, the Seahawks, one more disappointment on a reservation full of disappointment.* Jared had lost a carton of Marlboros on the last game the Hawks had lost.

Another guy was talking, holding the eagle feather, stroking it while he blubbered about losing his kids after a dope bust. He tipped his head back, exposing two or three missing teeth—a meth user, rocking fore and aft—shaking and crying for his little boys, now wards of tribal court.

Vision Quest—what a joke. Who could have vision in all this? What the hell was the point? Jared's mind kept up the cynical rhetoric.

He realized he was wandering again and tried to concentrate on the Circle. He hadn't had a drink or a hit in a while. Wasn't it time his thinking cleared up?

The Circle leader, Jimmy Dunn, a recovering alcoholic in his forties and a worker for Children's

Health Services, took the feather and gave some basic instruction to the group.

"It's important to you, to your families, to your tribe that you become clean and sober and trust-worthy individuals. Right now nobody can trust you. Your families don't trust you—you don't even trust each other. Everyone here has been ordered here, either by tribal court or state court. Do you guys realize that this is the last stop before prison?"

Yeah, the last stop before prison, as if life wasn't already a prison. Well, maybe just the last stop. His mind couldn't help but elaborate the obvious.

Jared thought back to the times he had stolen from his family, his mom, his uncles and cousins, in order to buy booze and dope. He had become a "coyote," not the sly trickster everyone loved and admired, but the dark thief, who used everyone he could. He had betrayed those who loved him, who had taken care of him when he was little. Jared had convictions for burglary, grand larceny, petty theft, possession of illegal substances, assault, and breaking-and-entering, not to mention a hand-ful of DUIs. He felt bad about it when sober and clean but didn't care at all when he was using. It amazed him that what was left of his family still loved him.

Late one rainy night Jared and a couple bud-dies broke into the tribally owned convenience store. They kicked in a side door and took several cases of beer, a case of cigarettes, and thirty-eight dollars in cash. Just as they were leaving with their loot, a tribal security guard came out of nowhere with a flashlight in his hand. Jared tackled him at the knees, knocking the wind out of the overweight man. Only then did he recognize his cousin Arnie. They made eye contact as Arnie lay retching on the rain-soaked ground; then Jared ran into the night.

Arnie had filed his report about the B and E and the assault, neglecting to identify any of the thieves. Jared never went to apologize to his cousin, even though he knew he should have. Cousin Arnie was in court the day Jared was sentenced, having been caught despite Arnie's incomplete report and sketchy details. He sat in the back of the courtroom, out of uniform, with tears running down his face.

The old circuit court judge had looked at Jared with disgust when he informed him, "One more conviction for anything and I will sentence you to hard time at Oregon State Penitentiary. As it is, I'm inclined to make you a guest of Lincoln County Jail for a period of thirty days. Remember what I just said about O-S-P. I mean it, Mr. Spotted-Horse." With that he dropped his gavel and Jared was escorted to jail, where he spent the next twenty-four days. He was released six days early for good behavior.

Lisa, the skinny, raven-haired meth-head beside Jared, was nodding her head as she rocked fore and aft like a dory boat crossing the bar: a typical tweeker motion that the "jonesers" coming off drugs and craving them couldn't help doing while drying out. Her kids were in foster care over in the Willamette Valley somewhere. She hadn't seen them in five weeks. Another three and she could have a supervised visit, if she stayed clean—the big "if."

The eagle feather materialized in Jared's left hand, as though landing. He looked down at it, stroked the fluffy tuft, soft in his hand at the base, then firming up and strengthening the farther his fingers moved toward the dark spots on the grey-white mottled tip. He closed his eyes as he spoke.

"I been here too many times, in this A and D stuff. I tried the white guy twelve-step but can't get past step two. I tried the dry-out center. I been through the program four or five times. My liver ain't right. The doc says I could get real sick this time if I don't quit usin' and drinkin'. I can feel it deep down in my guts—yeah … he's right on. I think I better get clean this time or there won't be no next time. Ya know what I mean? I could be lookin' at prison time too."

"I think my mind is beginnin' to clear up some. I dunno for sure though."

He perused his little audience to see if anyone had heard him. The meth gal rocked a "yes." The toother was looking down, maybe asleep. The Circle leader dutifully nodded that he, at least, understood. He then checked his watch with a quick flick of the wrist.

"I think maybe 'vision' is what I need to get. I need to make a vision, or, seek one, I guess." Jared stammered, unsure of the right words. He found himself sweating.

"Okay, on that note, 'vision', we'll close for today, the Circle leader said. "I'll see you guys tomorrow at seven p.m. right here. Don't forget to pick up your meds over at the pharmacy tomorrow if you need to." He inadvertently reached for the Camel straights showing through his shirt pocket, remembered the "no smoking in the clinic" rule, and headed for the side door to feed his craving for nicotine.

Jared eyed Lisa as she brushed by, heading for the pharmacy. She seemed to "brush by" a little closer than necessary. He wondered if she would be worth the trouble and decided that she probably wouldn't. He let her go, knowing he might regret it later but pretty sure he wouldn't. There had always been a little spark of attraction to her but he had never followed up. It just seemed like drama followed her around. She was beautiful, or at least had been, when they had gone to high school together. Then her drinking and carousing had gotten out of hand. She and Chucky had gotten together and had some kids. The marriage didn't last. Actually, Jared wasn't sure if they had ever been married or just shacked up. That seemed to be the way these days. Not too many of his peer group chose marriage. That sounded a lot like commitment. It was hard to be free and committed at the same time.

"Yep, best leave that one alone."

2

A True Friend

In the parking lot Jared lit up the half cigarette he had put out earlier and stashed atop his ear. It was dry and acrid but the hit was still there. He didn't smoke for flavor or even status, like he had as a kid. He smoked for the hit, the little high, that legal shot of lightheadedness that you only got if you didn't light up for an hour or so.

It was drizzling again in Siletz. Well, no surprise for the Oregon Coast. He wondered if it was raining down on the Rogue—Tolhut Tahilee (*tole hut! twaheelee*, "water flowing deep" in the Tututini language)—where his tribe had originally lived. *Now those guys had vision. They were masters of their own land in those days.*

Rick Blackhawker rumbled by; he honked and waved from his smoky rust-red Ford pickup with the yellow door. The driver's side window was duct-taped where the glass had been broken out. Another toothless warrior, thought Jared. Rick had always had that crooked Copenhagen grin, even as a kid.

Rick really wasn't missing all that many teeth. They were just so dark and tobacco stained that it looked like it, at least from a distance. *And distance is better,* he chuckled.

Jared tightened his oilskin horse-packer jacket as he hiked back to the trailer park. The packer wasn't all that warm but it gave the impression that he was a horse guy. He needed to project something. It had been a purchase last year at Goodwill. He had gotten there right after opening on a Monday and had scored the oilskin before it even made it to the rack. The best five bucks he had ever spent.

The trailer was cold. Some of the guys called them mobile homes, but Jared had always been brought up to call a spade a spade. He lit the propane stove burner to warm things up. The trailer didn't have a furnace anymore; it had died a couple winters back. The old landlord refused to fix it and had accused Jared of breaking it. Jared knew better than to push it. When renters had complained in the past, their rent had been raised.

The cooking stove worked OK most of the

time. When it didn't, he just used extra blankets. The coast weather was usually mild, seldom dropping below fifty degrees, even in winter. The occasional winter blast of snow and ice almost never lasted more than a week or so.

The roof was leaking again, dripping into well-placed cans and buckets on the floor. Jared made a mental note to get up there and smear another batch of black tar over the leaking areas. It usually took several applications to get through a normal winter. The water had stained the wall, leaving long dark streaks and blotches on the old wood paneling. There was a mold smell that never went away, even in the dry months of summer.

He turned on the old, dusty, wood-cabinet Magnavox television and noted that Oprah was struggling with a new wave of weight-loss longing. She was talking ever so sweetly to her studio audience, and of course the millions of TV listeners, about how we are fine "just the way we are." But how "much healthier and happier" we would be if we just dropped those extra twenty-five or thirty pounds … blah … blah … blah …

He changed the channel to *Walker, Texas Ranger. Now that has possibilities.* At least Walker had some sense of the Indians on the land, even though he went way over the top sometimes. *Too much noble warrior crap.*

A wave of snow and screen-squelch crackled as a gust of wind jostled the antenna. The signal from the Otter Crest station wasn't very strong but it was way better than the seventy-five bucks a month the cable company had charged before it so rudely cut off service for nonpayment several months ago.

Walker was driving his really cool pickup decked out with roll bar and overhead lights when Bobby Coons walked in with a six-pack of Pepsi—cans, not bottles.

"Hey Jare, how was Circle today?" He unsheathed a can and tossed it to Jared on the couch. "Any new women show up?" He popped one for himself and took a long swig of the cold, fizzy pop.

"Naw, nuthin' worth mentionin'. Lisa's back, but lookin' rough as ever. I think she's been over in Warm Springs. Haven't seen her in a while. Lookin' kinda like she been drug through a knot-hole backwards, ya know."

"Enit?"

"Yeah, enit." Bobby laughed at the old word that stood for "ain't it?" It seemed to be a universal tribal catchall. Then he looked quizzically toward Jared. "Heard she lost her kids again."

"Yep. Some stuff came up in Circle but I can't really talk about it."

"Yeah, okay. I get it. What gets said in Circle stays in Circle, like Vegas."

"Yep, just like Vegas, only no slots or tables. Speaking of, have you been down to the casino lately? Any action?"

Bobby knew Jared had lost more than one paycheck at the tribal casino, a sore subject with many of the tribal members. He was careful how he answered, not wanting to start his old school chum on a gambling binge.

"Same old stuff, lose a few then lose a few more …"

Bobby exhaled a healthy belch to illustrate his feigned disgust for the tribal casino even though both men knew that every year the casino handed out checks ranging between a thousand and fifteen hundred dollars to each tribal member. Last year Bobby had bought a new Winchester model 70 hunting rifle and a top-of-the-line Leupold scope with his check. Jared had blown his at the blackjack table in less than an hour. He was getting some help with these monkeys on his back, but he knew it was just a matter of time until he used again, either drinking or doping or gambling. His biggest fear was hurting his loved ones in order to support his bad habits. He kept pushing hopelessness to the back of his mind.

They finished watching *Walker;* then when *Walker* came on again Jared asked his old friend a question. "Ever think about going on Vision Quest? Ya know, like the old ones used to talk about?"

"Hmm. Yeah. I thought about it, but never tried it. I dunno, Jare—seems like that stuff quit workin' when the whites took over, way back on the Rogue, maybe before that. Seems like we just lost our medicine, know what I mean? That whole thing of goin' up on a mountain and seekin' the Great Spirit? The fastin' and prayin' and singin' and stuff? I wouldn't know how to do that even if I wanted to. I ain't even sure there is a Great Spirit. If there was one, he sure let our people down."

"I'm sure our tribe used to do that. I think some of that higher ground down on the Rogue was sacred. I'll bet if we went and looked we could find sign of the old bunch down there. Well, how long's it been since we come to the rez? Let's see, they got rounded up in eighteen fifty-five or so. There has to be some sign, some medicine still left over from the old days.

"Am I just pipe dreamin', Bobby?" He knew he sounded desperate. Well, he was desperate. The "medicine" Bobby mentioned meant "power" to tribal folks, or more accurately, "spiritual power." Jared had no spiritual power anymore and he knew it. He knew he would die because of his inability to control his own actions, his addictions, and it was killing him as surely as the sun rose in the east and went down in the west.

"What's all this crap about, Jare? Are you sick or somethin'?" Bobby could see the yellow in Jared's eyes, and he had a sinking feeling that his friend was sicker than he wanted to know.

"Are you okay, Skin?" Skin was short for Redskin, a common term of endearment on most reservations. This was despite the fact that the term had originated from the bounty money paid for salted scalps, ears, and foreskins turned red by sodium nitrate back in the old Indian-hunter days, a tradition established by the English and quickly adopted by the French.

"The doc told me I won't make it much longer if I can't stay clean. The liver and stuff ain't doin' so hot. Twenty-four years old and I could be dead from cirrhosis in a year or two. I know I promised Mom not to cuss anymore, just before she died, but that is horse shit! I'm just a kid, ya know? What the hell is wrong with me, anyway?"

Bobby just sat there in the old oak-wood rocker Jared had inherited from his mom, rocking and creaking as he spoke between sips of Pepsi. He didn't have an answer for him but felt compelled to try.

"Ya know, Jare, my auntie used to have a sayin'. She was a Christian, ya know—Pentecostal, constantly spoutin' that Bible stuff. I never held to it. But she was always sayin' this one thing all the time. 'The people perish without vision.' She said that all the time. I never did know what she meant. Maybe she was talkin' about what you been talkin' about. Maybe she meant Vision Quest. I dunno. That religious stuff never got me anyplace except slapped on the hands with a ruler for talkin' outta turn. But there must be somethin' to it. How about it, Skin? Enit?" Bobby grinned that two-bit grin of his that he saved for those times when he thought he had done or said something really special, or at least cute. He swigged his Pepsi, belched loudly, and glanced at the TV.

Walker did a world class spin-kick on a bad dude, then punched out the guy's partner with a left hook and a right cross. Wap! The black deputy slapped the cuffs on one of them and Walker cuffed the other. End of show. Cut to commercial.

"Who could I talk to? Seriously. I think I might be in trouble here, Bobby. I'm thinkin' I don't want to end up like Mom did, in a box in the ground up at Paul Washington."

Paul Washington Cemetery was on Government Hill in Siletz. It held the earthly remains of tribal folk going back to the earliest days on

22

the reservation. The old Indian Agency buildings had been constructed "on the hill" back in the late 1850s when the original Siletz Reservation had been established. They had since fallen down, replaced by a tribal community building and pow-wow grounds.

The Siletz Tribe was terminated in 1954. All reservation lands reverted to the United States Government for sale and dispersement to government agencies and timber companies. The old cemetery on Government Hill fell into disrepair. The rock-hewn headstones tilted and became weather-chipped through the dark winters that followed, sharing a fate similar to the tribal people. The blackberry vines slowly covered some of the graves, hiding their deterioration from the outside world.

Then, in 1977, through no small effort of a handful of tribal leaders and their political allies, the tribe was restored and took the form of the Confederated Tribes of Siletz Indians of Oregon. The "restored" tribe went in and cleaned up the old cemetery, straightened up old headstones, cut brambles, trimmed grass, and planted flowers. Order and hope were restored through the hard work, prayers, and vision of those mighty warriors of valor.

Today, the Siletz Tribe has a land base of nearly

ten thousand acres, most of which is timberland.

The cemetery was named after Paul Washington, a Siletz tribal member who had died in World War I. He served honorably and was killed in action, protecting the only home he had ever known, America.

3

Mom

Doris Palmer, Jared's mom, was known as a wild girl around the logging/rez town. She became pregnant as a teenager and gave birth to Jared on a cool October morning. She named Tom Spotted-Horse as the father even though he had since left for Oregon State Penitentiary after convictions for domestic assault, attempted murder, assault on a police officer, and resisting arrest. He got twelve years with possibility of parole in seven. Neither Doris nor Jared ever heard from Tom again. Rumor had it that he had been paroled out, absconded to Pine Ridge Reservation, and disappeared after a drug raid went bad, resulting in the death of an FBI agent and a couple of suspects. Who knew? Who cared?

Doris struggled with alcohol for years. She

succumbed to "cirrhosis of the liver due to chronic alcoholism," or so read the death certificate, when Jared was eighteen. He knew it meant she just plain drank herself to death. Truth be known, she died of a broken heart.

As Jared talked with Bobby, he thought back to the three or four months preceding his mother's death. She was in tribal housing, lying in bed, unable to do much besides breathe and sleep. Her body was overstuffed, like a teddy bear gone horribly bad. Her skin was blotchy yellow with black smears that looked like bruises. Some were green. Some gray. Her eyes were a yellow-brown that made Jared think of rotten teeth. Her breathing, cold and raspy, reeked of death.

When she did wake up she always asked for a drink. Anything to "knock down the pain." He couldn't help himself. He gave her wine, whiskey, vodka, beer, whatever he could get his hands on. He learned a term later, in his own trail of recovery. That term haunted him to this day: *enabler*. He was an enabler, a coyote, a doer of bad things to the people. A trickster. Damn that word! Coyote! Enabler!

He remembered the day she died. She had just messed the bed again. He left the room to get some fresh air before going back in to clean her up for the hundredth time. He spent quite a while getting air, stalling around, listening to the river bubbling down at the riffle below the house. He went back in, only to discover that she was gone, crossed over—to where, he didn't know.

She died at thirty-five and he never mourned her; he couldn't. He went through the motions with his aunties and uncles, friends, and the old white minister who said she would rest with angels. And she was put into the cold wet ground up at Paul Washington, hopefully deep enough that the frost wouldn't cause her to shiver in winter. To mourn was to honor the dead. To grieve was to suffer their loss in an open and healing way. Jared did neither.

Damn, he thought, realizing he had broken the no-cuss promise again. A couple of months before she died he had promised her he would quit cussing, or at least cut way down. He had tried to keep that promise but struggled constantly with it. How could a logger not cuss? Jack never cussed. He got just as beat up as everyone else did too. Logging was a tough and physical game. Anyway, it's not like his mom didn't cuss. She could put a sailor to shame with her mouth.

Later he thought, *She perished without a vision too. Damn.*

4

The New Kid

Jared had met Tim Simms in Mr. Thompson's fifth grade class. Mr. Thompson was a good teacher, strict but fair, who liked to teach "out of the box," especially when it came to history and politics. He was one of the few teachers who were willing to fly in the face of contemporary teaching when necessary, especially when it came to Native American history; but when it came to matters of discipline and order, he took no prisoners.

Tim Simms was introduced to the class as a new student one fall morning after school had been going for a month or so. As a late transfer, he was "the new kid" in class. He had red hair and blue eyes and was of average height. He was as tall as Jared but only weighed fifty-seven pounds, as opposed to Jared's sixty-three. He looked like a good fit for the Siletz class, a mix of Indians and whites reflecting the ethnic makeup of a logging town in what most would call "Indian Country."

Tim immediately zeroed in on Jared at the first recess of the day. Bobby, Jared, and a couple other boys were shooting marbles in the sand when Tim kicked some of that sand into the circle and into the faces of three of the boys, including Jared. The two exchanged harsh words—"What are you red Injuns doin' down there in the dirt?"—but didn't get into a fist fight since teachers were watching. Still, they both knew that they weren't friends at first sight. It was understood that they would have to settle their differences in the way most boyhood differences were settled in those days, in that place: with their fists.

They stayed away from each other for the next week or so. Jared was a pretty good boxer, having been trained in the Golden Gloves program for several years. A lack of funding and public outcry against the sport brought the program to its inevitable close. He didn't miss it all that much though; he didn't enjoy hitting people any more than he enjoyed getting hit.

It happened on a Tuesday afternoon when Mr. Thompson stepped out of the classroom to go to the office. Tim, or Timmy as some had begun to call him, and Big Fred, a slow-witted boy much larger than most whom Tim had befriended immediately, moved menacingly toward Robert Bagay, who was small for his age. Timmy pushed him into Big Fred, who was dutifully waiting on all fours behind him, as though the sneak move had been practiced before. Robert went down with a crash, breaking his coke-bottle glasses on the edge of a desk. He screamed in pain as his head hit the concrete floor.

The crashing noise was the first awareness Jared had of the lopsided situation. He was at the front of the class and had to turn in his desk chair to see what the commotion was. Robert, who had been a friend since first grade, was trying to get up and find his glasses at the same time. Big Fred kicked him in the belly and knocked him back to the floor.

Later, Jared couldn't recall crossing the room. His next remembrance was of his fist connecting with Timmy's chin, followed by several quick and well-placed blows to the jaw, chin, and nose. Amazingly, Tim never went down or lost his balance. He did attempt to cover; he even managed to duck a right cross. The next blow, a left hook, landed squarely on Tim's cheekbone. Jared followed that one with a right jab that made a popping sound as it dislocated his opponent's nose.

Blood was now splattering with each blow.

The screams could be heard clear down in the principal's office, where Mr. Thompson and Mr. Pool were having a cup of coffee and discussing the upcoming afternoon assembly. They both ran the full length of the hall with their imaginations running wild as to what catastrophe could have befallen their poor little students. Thompson was the first to the classroom door and saw Timmy duck under a right cross that Jared had thrown. He couldn't believe what he was seeing. The whole class was in a state of riot. Ben Shakley had Big Fred in a headlock. Two of the best girl students in class were hitting each other with three-ring binders. Two other boys were rolling on the floor and throwing punches as fast and hard as they could. Ann Filman was standing on the teacher's desk screaming at the top of her lungs.

"Stop! Stop this instant!" roared Mr. Thompson, clapping his hands together and striding rapidly into the middle of the room just as Jared kneed Tim in the groin. Mr. Pool helped, separating fighting boys and girls as he stepped into the fray. Mr. Thompson shouted, "Now, someone tell me what is going on here!" Several students, mostly girls, started talking at once. "One at a time, please!" he yelled, a little calmer than before. Again they all started talking. "Okay, okay.

Jared, Ben, Fred, and you, new kid, Simms, go to the office right now! The rest of you sit down and shut up!"

Mr. Thompson set a quick pace down the hall, with himself in front of the little pack and Mr. Pool behind, making sure none of them strayed off. Jared had never seen a homelier man than Mr. Pool, the principal. He was a big man with a military crew cut, tall and broad-shouldered with a nose that had been broken and never properly set. Of course, as a boy, Jared never knew why the nose was crooked; he just knew that it was and it was scary to him.

All the boys received a good paddling and were suspended from school for three days. Jared and Bobby spent those days down on the river trying to catch fish, with Bobby catching most of them and making fun of Jared the whole time.

After the fight, Timmy came to Jared; they talked and shook hands. They were fast friends after that and were considered the two toughest boys in the class, if not in the whole school. Tim quit picking on the smaller kids after that. He had a new friend and didn't want to disappoint him since Jared tried to live honorably. Timmy had never experienced that before. He didn't know if that was an "Indian thing" or a "Jared thing." He realized in his fifth-grade heart that Jared was a friend worth having. Timmy even joined sports so he could hang out with his new friend.

Timmy's dad was what most would call a red-neck. He had no use for the college-educated, the blacks, the Democrats, or the Indians. He had always made his living with his hard hat, caulk boots, gloves, the sweat of his brow, and a can-do attitude. George Simms was the woods boss for the biggest logging company around. He was respected, even feared, by the men who worked for him. He had proven himself worthy by work-ing and surviving for years in the harsh elements of the Pacific Coast Range, working in some of the nastiest weather and steepest hillsides known to man. He started as a lowly choker-setter, then worked his way up through the ranks: chaser, rig-ging slinger, hook-tender, all-around equipment operator, timber faller, siderod and finally, woods boss. George had done this by working hard and steady. He earned a reputation as someone who could "get wood." To say he was a tough egg would greatly understate the reality of the man.

Timmy knew his dad was tough. He seldom saw him; George was up and gone hours before daybreak and didn't usually get home until well after dark. Then he was immediately on the phone, directing the next day's trucking and log-ging operating plans. He had no time for Timmy and they both knew it. George tried to make time for Timmy and his sister but just couldn't seem to make it happen. He suspected he would regret that someday but just didn't have time to think about it much.

Timmy hung out with Jared and Bobby when he could. He liked the way Uncle Ree oversaw the efforts of the young boys in their attempts to hunt, fish, and trap. He was amazed at how Bobby could catch more fish than anyone else, but he was doubly amazed when he saw Bobby try to shoot a deer or an elk. It just didn't happen for him. As good as Bobby was at fishing, he made up for it when hunting. Jared and Timmy teased him good-naturedly, enjoying the fact that Bobby wasn't able to beat them at everything.

Jared was a natural hand at trapping. He could set "water sets" for beaver, muskrat, and otter that usually caught fur. He was also good at catching bobcats and coyotes. The coyotes didn't bring much money but the bobcats did, especially if they were "prime," having long hair in the coldest part of winter.

They all took part in skinning and stretching and drying the pelts; they all shared in the sale of the furs too.

Timmy had never been part of such a crew before. He began to understand that it was possible to harvest from the land and love it at the same time. Ree always took the time to explain that Creator gave the animals, plants, air, and water to us in order to feed and shelter us. It was up to us to be grateful and to show respect.

Jared had been young then. He tried to remember what Ree had taught them but when the drugs and alcohol came into his life it was like a whirlwind of bad medicine. He had grown into a man who had lost something; he wondered if it was his soul.

5

Euchre Mountain

Jared woke early the next morning, took care of his bathroom business, and got ready to catch the "crummy." He wolfed down a stale doughnut and knew he could balance out the sugar crash with coffee during the day. He threw a couple of bologna sandwiches together and grabbed another doughnut for his lunch. He was going to have to go to the store before work tomorrow since he had to use the heels of the bread. He never had liked them much.

"Crummy" was the name loggers used to describe the crew bus that picked them up before daybreak every morning. Jared was a logger, a choker-setter by trade—a "grunt." He was one of the guys who wrapped cold, wet, stiff cable around rough-barked logs on muddy hillsides day after rainy day. As choker-setters go, he was a pretty good one, when he showed up sober and not too hung over.

He knew his job had been on the line lately. He'd missed quite a bit of work and had heard about it from the siderod—the logging boss—who was supportive of Jared pursuing treatment rather than his old pursuit of the bottle. Jared knew in his heart that the next time he missed work without calling in he would be looking for another job. Considering the pain he felt day after day, it might be for the best. Maybe a mill job would be easier on his guts. He was really tired of hurting all the time. He knew the doc had been right about his liver.

The crummy pulled up in the predawn darkness and honked a quick shave-and-a-hair-cut. Jared grabbed his old beater oil–stained canvas backpack, with his caulk boots—spike-soled boots for walking on logs—lunch pail, gloves, hard hat, and raingear stuffed into it, and headed out the door. He climbed into the smoke-filled crummy and found a seat. He stretched his Romeo-slippered feet out for a half-hour snooze while the bus bumped its way up Euchre Mountain to the job site. It was raining hard. The windshield wipers squeaked as they swished left and right in an apparent attempt to hypnotize Jared.

Old Pete, the driver, who was also the donkey puncher, wearing his customary red felt hat, hickory shirt, and red "Loggers World" suspenders attached to Frisco jeans, nodded a greeting and took a quick drag on his cigarette. He then shifted into first and took off, balancing a thermos cup in his right hand and steering with his left, the ever-present Lucky Strike dangling from his lip. He wore a two-day stubble of beard and was shod in lace-up boots that served him well for landing work and running the donkey. He was what most loggers would call an "all-around hand."

Jared couldn't nap this morning as he customarily did along with the other half dozen occupants sprawled or slumped in the bowels of the crummy. He had experienced too many weird thoughts and dreams lately, since "sobering up." It was as though a dead part of him was coming back to life.

He looked through the mud-crusted window hoping to spy an elk as the daylight crept through the timber and onto the scattered clear-cuts. He had seen a small herd last week, feeding their way out of the tall Douglas fir and Western hemlock, heads-down hungry, cropping grass and browsing as they moved across an opening toward another stand of dark timber—the "tall and uncut" as the old donkey puncher called it. A small bull and a few cows and calves seeking that last-minute meal before retiring to heavy cover for the daylight hours.

It seemed to Jared that elk and alcoholics had something in common. They were both nocturnal: most of their activity took place under cover of darkness and they hid and slept during the daylight hours. He thought about his family members who had gone into the long sleep as a result of alcohol and drugs—too many to count—too many faces that had blurred off into memory and then faded from even that. He didn't like thinking about it but he just couldn't help it.

Some were off in prison, serving sentences for everything from murder to child abuse. Maybe the lucky ones were in the ground. Or maybe the really lucky ones were in the prisons, sitting in dry and warm cells, not out on some muddy hillside with some siderod yelling down the hill for "more wood, dammit!" Siderods weren't employed because of their ability to make friends. They were there to get logs, and lots of them. Those who did, stayed. Those who didn't—well, they went somewhere else.

The crummy took a bad bounce as it hit a chuckhole, eliciting a "son of a bitch!" from the driver as steaming hot coffee burned into his knee. Jared chuckled to himself, enjoying the cheap sideshow at the grizzled driver's expense.

They pulled onto the landing. The donkey puncher and the log processor operator exited the crummy and slogged through the mud to their machines to start them up and get things under way. The loader operator, who was also the siderod, had been on the job for a couple of hours already, loading the first string of log trucks in the dark.

The "rigging crew," of which Jared was a member, came fully awake to the sounds of diesel engines and loader grapples snapping hard steel in the dark. They got busy rustling up caulk boots and raingear. One of the guys in the back farted so loudly and raunchily that a fistfight broke out. "Outside, you idiot! Damn, Franky, can't you wait a minute? You're a real pig, you know that!"

Smack! Smack! A door was kicked open and Franky rolled out into the cold mud, rubbing his eye and cussing, spitting what looked suspiciously like blood and Copenhagen mixed together. He cooled off when the siderod yelled to "get over the hill and quit screwing around!" It didn't take long for the rest of the boys to get outside and start down the mud-slicked hillside.

Jared thought back to the time when he, Uncle Ree, and his mom had taken a canoe trip across Tachenich Lake. It was a warm July morning, beautiful, with an east wind blowing the mayflies out onto the water. The trout and bass were feeding on them, voracious in their appetites. Ree handed Jared his old Fenwick fly rod and showed him how to false cast, then strip line and cast a little further. He hooked trout, bass, and bluegill that morning, more than he could count. Ree netted them and Doris threaded them onto the stringer. She laughed until she cried when Jared slapped Ree on the side of the head with a big slimy bass. Ree good-naturedly threatened Jared with a free swimming lesson. They all had a great laugh over it.

Later that afternoon they paddled back to camp with Ree teaching Jared the J-stroke. It felt like life just couldn't get any better. They built a small campfire and fried fish with potatoes and onions. They ate watermelon and drank coffee so black it left a mark on your tongue.

Ree and Doris showed Jared how to make little teepees out of sticks, then hang wires with fish on them and smoke the fish over a fire. His first attempts were not pretty, but after a fashion he could smoke fish to perfection with his newfound skill. He had to get the right amount of salt, the right size fire, and the proper amount of time; if he did all this just right, his fish were delicious. He got quite good at this over the years and won the praise of many tribal elders.

Jared was eleven years old. This day on the water took place during one of Doris's few sobering-up periods. She was sober for almost six months. During that time Jared got to know his mom and she got to know him. In later years he would remark, "I would give my left arm to have those six months back."

Franky, Jack, and Jared were the three choker-setters. They worked well together most of the time and got lots of logs out. Franky was pretty quiet, at least until he got a few beers in him; then he exhibited a fine sense of humor. He wrote notes and little poems on paper napkins for the barmaids downtown. He never really got anywhere with them, but his writings sure made for hilarious reading at times.

One of the barmaids down on the water-front had started calling him "Milton." Everyone thought it must be because of the little poems but no one knew for sure. Anyway, Franky was going to ask her out one of these days but hadn't got around to it yet. He was a great one for writing notes but not much for talking to the ladies. He just couldn't get his nerve up.

Jack was an ex-hippie-Jesus-freak-turned-log-ger. Every little thing was about Jesus. He could see Jesus in the clouds and Jesus in the air. He claimed he could talk to Jesus and Jesus would answer him back. The crew got really sick of hearing about Jesus so they told Jack to keep all that to himself and just do his job, set his choker, and keep his damn mouth shut.

He was more than a little hurt, but he did stop the preaching and got into the logging more. He really was a good guy who would give you the shirt off his back if you ever needed it. Of course, he was the smallest guy on the crew so his shirt wouldn't fit anybody but himself.

When Jack first came out he wasn't much of a logger. He even showed up his first day on the job wearing tennis shoes and jeans. He could hardly set a choker on flat ground, let alone drag one up the hillside and set a tough one. He kept trying though. He started dressing in logging clothes with proper boots and gloves. Brad was tempted day after day to can him because he slowed the rest of the boys down. But like most loggers, he just couldn't fire a man who tried with all he had. So Jack stayed on and fought the good fight.

Over time he became a good man and a friend to everyone on the crew. More importantly, he showed up every day, sober and on time. He had earned their respect, which was never an easy task with working loggers. Respect was earned; it was never, ever, a gift.

Jared had gotten into the habit of lacing up his caulk boots really tight first thing so he wouldn't sprain an ankle going downhill in the semi-darkness every morning. This crew liked to get an early start so they could get off early. They single-filed down through the broken limbs, loosened boulders, and trenched mud, talking little with the exception of the occasional cuss word after tripping and falling.

Brad was in charge of the actual log hooking. He was the rigging slinger, the guy who picked which logs to hook to make up the "turn" of logs to ship to the landing each time the rigging came back. The rigging, made up of several chokers or hooking cables, came back every three minutes or so. The choker-setters scrambled in to grab the chokers and set them each onto individual logs. When the drop line was tightened and pulled up onto the "skyline carriage," the combined tree-length logs in the chokers, sometimes as many as five or six, made up a full turn and were pulled to the landing with the skidding line, moving as fast as thirty to forty miles per hour.

This went on hour after hour, day after day, month after month. Jared, Frank, Jack, Brad, and the rest of the crew struggled to get through each day without getting hurt, maimed, or even killed. Getting hurt wasn't that unusual. It could happen anytime but was usually the result of someone doing something stupid.

One choker-setter had broken a leg after falling off a log pile and landing on a boulder. It took the rigging crew nearly two hours to pack him out on the stretcher to the waiting ambulance up on the landing. He survived it but never did walk without a limp after that. His hip was broken and the ball joint was crushed. A couple of surgeries later he retired from logging and took up regular residence in the local bars. He now referred to himself as an "officially retired honky-tonk logger." To hear him tell it, he had been the finest logger ever to hit the Pacific Coast.

Sometimes skyline logging, especially in winter, felt to Jared like a war zone. The danger was constant. The work was hard and thankless. And for those who got hurt there was no Purple Heart, just a little time off at half pay until healed. Then it was back to the same muddy hillside for more hard thankless work.

But sometimes in the spring and summer the work was downright fun. When the sun came out, the guys could shed their rain gear, the mud dried up, footing was good and stable, and logging became a game. Quite a few of the guys on the crew were Siletz Indians, and as everybody knows, Indians love to play games, sometimes very dangerous ones. Brad was part Siletz and part Irish and who knows what else. Alfred, up on the landing, was Siletz and Warm Springs. Racial teasing took place almost as much as talking about women did. It was an accepted means of passing the day away and usually done in a friendly way, but occasionally it led to harsh words and a fistfight.

Brad played a game called "run or die." The rules were simple: when the last guy got his choker set, Brad would tip up his "bug" and blow the whistle, which was simply a transmitted radio signal from the bug to the receiver on the yarder or donkey. The signal then triggered an air whistle, which could be heard for miles. The donkey puncher engaged the clutches and began hoisting the logs into the air and toward the suspended carriage. The crew had to scramble like mad to get in the clear before those logs started smacking together and were hoisted up hundreds of feet and then reeled to the landing. The average turn of logs weighed about ten thousand pounds. When something broke and they fell from the sky, there was hell to pay.

To make things even more exciting, any crew caught playing run or die was immediately fired. And if safety inspectors ever witnessed such a dangerous practice, that logging job would be shut down, fined thousands of dollars, and probably put out of business.

Jared knew he was too sick to play those kinds

of games anymore. He had thrown up that morning on the way down the hill. He was weak and short of breath and had cold sweats. He hadn't had a drink in weeks and was disappointed that he wasn't healing faster. He suspected that he wasn't quick enough to survive the logging game and made no bones about telling Brad, Jack, and Franky when the suggestion came up.

"Boring" was Franky's reply, but no more was said about it. They knew he was sick too.

The crummy ride home that night wasn't unusual at all. The rigging crew slept, with the exception of old Pete, who balanced coffee, cigarette, steering wheel, and gearshift while managing to live through the whole ordeal. Jared always suspected Pete's "coffee" of having more additives than cream and sugar. The old donkey puncher did love his whisky. But Jared never said a word because Pete's brother-in-law owned the outfit. Whiskey or not, Pete was one hell of an operator, in Jared's opinion.

6

Fire in the Hole!

Jared thought of Timmy, who had joined the Marine Corps right out of high school. Timmy had tried to talk Jared into going too, but Jared was on probation for breaking into the gas station and stealing beer. It fouled up his chance to get into the military. The recruiter had told him, "Keep your nose clean, get off probation, and then come see me."

He was off probation a week when he got busted for drunk driving. That pretty much ruined his chances of getting into the Corps. He had really wanted to join up with Tim, but it couldn't happen now. He recounted some of the good times he, Bobby, and Tim had had over the years. Jared and Tim could've been "the Indian and the White Guy." They were about the same size. Tim was

Anglo, with red hair and freckles. Jared was dark haired and olive skinned, with the classic high cheekbones of the Indian. Yet, they were good friends. Jared missed his red-headed, freckled friend and thought of him often. They exchanged letters occasionally, mostly around the holidays, but neither was good at writing.

Tim came home after boot camp with lots of big stories about the hard work and deprivation of Marine Corps training. Jared and Bobby had a million questions as they sat by the campfire drinking Bud that first night.

It occurred to Jared that he had no better friends than Bobby and Tim. They were both good and loyal to him and had both proven it many times throughout their boyhood.

He remembered the time when he and Tim were hunting up on Table Mountain. Jared tried to cross a gully by walking on a log that had fallen across it, making a natural bridge. The trouble was, the bridge was slick with rain and moss. He was halfway across when his feet slipped and he fell into the rocky gully bottom, breaking his right ankle so badly that the bone was sticking out. Tim splinted the ankle and helped him up onto the trail to the pickup, piggybacking him across the rougher areas and creeks. As it was, they barely made it back to the truck before a bad storm hit.

Jared shuddered to think what would have happened to him had Tim not been there. He knew he would've gotten a fire going and survived the night; but oh what a miserable night it would have been with a broken ankle and no real shelter. A fire will keep a man alive as long as he can retrieve wood for it. At some point the wood would've been too far to fetch with a bad leg. Thinking back on the matter, he knew it could have gone either way.

Jared finally dozed in the steam and cigarette smoke as the crummy bounced down the mountain. Brad was slouched into his seat, snoring already. Franky sighed deeply and sprawled out on the backseat, his wet rain gear on the seat next to him, mud caked and drying slowly.

The crummy swerved to miss a boulder in the road. Jared woke up and realized he had been dreaming of Lisa. "Wow! Where did that come from?" At least he was feeling a little better.

They were almost to town when Jared took stock of who was awake and who wasn't. Franky was sound asleep. Brad was semi-comatose. Jack was truly out cold. Jared slipped the lighter out of his shirt pocket and fired it up. Jack's stagged-off jeans had about three inches of fringe hanging off the cuff. He'd cut the pants off above the seam, allowing them to tear away if they got hung up on

51

brush in a dangerous situation such as a log rolling downhill toward him. The fringe was also perfect kindling and served as such when Jared touched the flame to it. It immediately flared up, creating a tough situation for Jack. He woke with a start and began slapping his legs, trying to put the fire out and screaming "Jesus, help me! Help me, Jesus!"

Pete yelled back, "Knock it the hell off, you damn baboons! I'm tryin' to drive here!" Harsh as all that sounded, Pete was grinning. He had been a rigging man once himself, a few decades back. He had always considered rigging men as half baboon and half human, with the baboon being the smart half, himself exempted of course.

About that time the flames flared right up Jack's leg where he had spilled the saw gas on them earlier. He did a wild jump and ended up smacking into old Pete's back, causing him to swerve and run down a "Dangerous Road" sign. He recovered control about the same time Franky and Brad threw their coffee and pop on Jack. It was a noisy mess resembling a Keystone Kops movie, but the fire and the crummy were brought under control at last. The lukewarm coffee and sugary soda ran in patterns on the mud-crusted rubber floor mats.

Everybody got a good laugh at Jack's expense, with no one owning up to the attempted arson. Jared's stop came up and he jumped out with the parting words, "I enjoyed the weenie roast, fellas! Try to keep 'er in the road, Pete!"

Neither Jack nor Pete acknowledged him but drove off toward the shop, leaving him standing in the exhaust smoke of the dented-up crummy.

7

Thinking of the Rogue

Bobby dropped by after work to watch *Walker*. It was another good guy–bad guy scenario, with Walker and his deputy whupping up on the bad guys as usual.

"Hey, I got a postcard from Timmy. He's in Fort Bragg. Gonna be shipped out in a couple weeks. Said to tell you 'howdy.'" Bobby held the card out for Jared, who took it.

"Got Circle tonight, Bro?" inquired Bobby.

"Yeah. Ninety meetings in ninety days. I'm on thirty-four," replied Jared as he read the postcard.

"Man, that's a lot of frickin' meetings. Ain't you sick of it yet? I mean, that is one hell of a bunch of meetings. I don't know if I could hack it, ya know?"

"Yeah, I been thinkin' about splittin' outa

here. Too much Circle, too much BS for this Skin. Maybe we could slip over to Warm Springs or down to the Rogue. Always warmer down on the Rogue, enit?"

"Enit!"

Jared had a redeeming quality that was one reason Bobby, all 265 pounds of him, hung out at Jared's place: he could cook. He had the ability to make a good meal out of most anything, and if given a little meat or fish, he could work wonders. He also liked to hunt. He had been on probation so much that he wasn't allowed to hunt anymore but he went along with Bobby and his Uncle Ree when they went. Even when he couldn't shoot a rifle he was a good meat packer. They had scored on a couple bucks and a small bull elk last fall, and Jared had frozen steaks from them and canned the rest of his share.

He popped open a home-canned jar of venison and dropped the meat into a cast iron frying pan, lightly greased with real butter. The pan had been his mother's. He allowed his mind to drift back to better days when his mom's small, tanned hands had prepared meals for him. He added some wild onions he had picked in a dry creek bed and dried earlier in the year. He then proceeded to slice some green bell peppers, fresh chanterelle mushrooms—which he had picked at work that day—and potatoes into the stir-fry, adding some lemon pepper seasoning and a little garlic salt. Just before it was done, he dropped a quarter cup of hot water into the pan and put the lid on, shutting off the heat and letting it steam. He grabbed a stained dish cloth and swiped at a bit of dried spaghetti sauce on the old stained stove top.

Bobby sat by the TV with his mouth watering from the smells coming from the little kitchen ten feet from the old threadbare couch. *That boy will make somebody a fine wife someday*, he chuckled silently to himself.

"Chow's on. Eat or go hungry, big guy," bawled Jared. He didn't have to say it twice.

They dished up on some chipped plates that his mom had owned and emptied the pan, washing the food down with ice-cold Pepsi in a can, Bobby's contribution to supper.

Jared had cooked all his life, starting as a little kid. When most kids fended for themselves while the folks were on a toot somewhere, they were glad to eat cold cereal or pop tarts, even buttered toast. Not Jared. He had looked through his mom's cookbooks, watched cooking shows on TV, experimented on his own, and come out the other end a fair to middlin' camp cook, although he had spent little time in any kind of camp with the exception of hunting camp every fall.

"Ya know, Jare, if you was better lookin' and would take a bath once in a while, I'd consider movin' in, good as you cook." Bobby's parting re-mark earned him the wet dish rag in the back of the head as he ducked out the door to go home. He crunched away in the fresh hail, rubbing the back of his head and picking at pieces of soggy spaghetti, his footfalls fading into the darkness and the evening cold.

"Anytime, big guy, anytime," Jared grinned at the insult, wondering if the quality of insults would improve given time and feeling a little like that funny guy Rodney Dangerfield, who "gets no respect." Dangerfield Junior. He couldn't help but grin at the imaginary picture of himself straight-ening a necktie and looking all bug-eyed and homely.

He and Bobby had been close since early child-hood, next door neighbors in the tribal housing project. They caught the bus together from first grade on. The two friends played sports together. Bobby was a good lineman on the football team, usually playing guard while Jared played running back, one of the "glory boys," as Mr. Gilman, the line coach, called the backfield. Basketball wasn't a sport either enjoyed since Bobby was slow and Jared was short. They sat that one out and hunted and fished in midwinter. Uncle Ree showed them how to set a trapline for beaver, otter, raccoon, and bobcats. They made good money in winter, selling the furs and were able to buy school clothes and, of course, more traps and ammunition. Jared bought a "squash blossom" necklace (large turquoise stones in heavy silver setting) for his mom for Christmas one year. She wore it to all the tribal ceremonies and functions after that, much to Jared's liking.

8

Bobby

Bobby's childhood had been a living hell. His old man came and went with the seasons; he worked the farms and orchards in the Willamette Valley during the summer and early fall as a picker. He didn't send much money home but usually sent something. When he came home he was flush with cash and always in a partying mood. Money and alcohol are a form of "honey to flies" on the rez. When Bob senior came home, his old "friends" came out of the woodwork. Young Bobby had many memories of Bob dancing with his mother to Willie Nelson, Waylon Jennings, Johnny Cash, and of course, George Jones. They broke out Credence Clearwater Revival when the party really got rolling.

Missy, Bobby's mom, loved to party too. They

had tons of fun while the money lasted, which usually wasn't long. When it ran out, so did the friends. The house would become tomblike except for the sounds of the TV and old Bobby's snoring as he slept off the binge.

Some of Bobby's earliest memories were of waking up in the morning to the stale smell of cigarettes, spilled beer, wine, and vomit. He didn't mind too much because he could step around the snoring partiers, some clothed, some not, and find leftover pizza, chips, and pop that had been used for mixer. He tried the beer and wine while the snoring was the only sound in the room, but he just didn't like the taste of it.

After one party that lasted several days, Bobby scored some potato salad and cold hot dogs. He got himself ready for school, caught the bus, and made it to school only to get deathly sick and be rushed to the hospital. He was diagnosed with food poisoning, most likely from the potato salad, which was several days old and laced with mayonnaise and eggs, both of which had turned to poison. His stomach was pumped and the contents were analyzed. He never cared much for potato salad after that, but he still had a liking for hot dogs.

Oftentimes, toward the end of an evening of partying after the crowd had gone home or passed out, Bob beat Missy to a pulp. He accused her of whoring around and being a nagging bitch. She wore her scars well, hiding them with makeup and scarves. But she couldn't hide the welts over her eyes or the crooked nose after he broke it. She limped most days because of her untreated back injuries. Once he broke her ribs by throwing her into a chest of drawers. She coughed up blood for nearly a week before she sought treatment at the emergency room in town. The nurse asked her who beat her up. She replied that she had taken a bad fall off a horse.

When the doctor examined Missy he asked her about the broken nose, the scars, and the limp. She said she had been a horse trainer for years and had suffered many a mishap as a result. The doctor exchanged a knowing glance with the ER nurse, shrugged it off. "No telling with these war hoops. They kill each other at random. What a waste."

The good doctor had treated and released so many of the Siletz people that he had become hardened toward anyone tribal. Their abuse toward one another, particularly to family members and spouses, was hard for him to fathom. Yet, when they came into emergency all beaten and bleeding inside and out, he did his best for them even though he knew he couldn't fix their real problem. He couldn't even define what their "real problem" was. He just knew that as a people the Siletz Tribe was sick and maybe getting sicker. He was tired of them coming in and asking him to apply band-aids when they required major surgery, speaking as to a whole race of people. He knew their social problems were astronomical. "God help me. For a fun-loving Irishman I sure have become a hard case."

Doctor Minton could remember ten years ago when he had finished his residency at Oregon Health Science University; he had thought of himself as a healer, someone who could do some good. He had considered becoming a missionary doctor, but having a wife and a child on the way precluded missionary work. He had accepted a position with the Newport Hospital, partly because of its proximity to the Siletz reservation but mostly because it was right on the Pacific Ocean. He had considered the plight of the Native Americans, the First Nations People, and had a desire to serve these folks who had suffered so much and so long at the hands of the European invasion.

Looking back, he felt foolish, as though he had been a starry-eyed optimist, a kid with so little idea of what these people were really like—or what people in general were really like. The Siletz were their own worst enemy, destroying each other at every opportunity, using alcohol as their chosen medium of death. Nowadays meth was competing for a close second in the death-and-destruction derby. "God forgive me. I think I've lost my way, my purpose."

He mulled these things as he noted Missy sitting on the examining table, dress torn, blackened eye, a cut and swollen lip. One of her front teeth was broken off at the gum line. He detected a gurgling sound in his stethoscope, indicating another broken rib and a possible lung laceration, perhaps even a full puncture.

She refused an x-ray because the old superstitions forbade the procedure (she made that part up, knowing he wouldn't push it if he thought it was a tribal religious taboo), so he patched her up as best he could, taking extra care to protect the rib cage area, gave her a prescription for pain meds, and sent her home with instructions for at least a week of complete bed rest.

Doctor Minton had begun leaving his hospital shift and going directly to Mickey's Bar for happy hour. He knew drinking wasn't the answer to his lost dreams but a little red-eye after a hard day at work wasn't such a terrible sin. Besides, he hadn't had a wife to go home to for five years now and he only got to see the kids every other weekend. He ordered a double Crown Royal on the rocks that showed up almost instantly.

9

Fishing

Bobby had the uncanny knack of catching fish when no one else could, even when the fish weren't biting. And when the fish were biting, he really cleaned up, catching three fish to Jared's one. Jared had often wondered if the reason was what that old commercial salmon fisherman had told him years ago. He had said that everyone has electricity in their body, some a big charge, some a little, some almost none. Those with just the right amount—say a quarter volt or so—project that charge onto their fishing rod, down the line, and to the hook. Fish are attracted, supposedly, by the electricity and bite out of some reflex. The old guy told it for gospel. Over the years Jared had watched Bobby work his magic and wondered if it were true.

One day in early fall, when the river was teeming with fish, Jared, Bobby, and Tim had cut sophomore class and gone down to the Bulls Bag hole. The Chinooks were in heavy and hungry as well. Bobby put five fish on the bank before Jared or Tim hooked a single one. Bobby cackled that loud laugh of his because six fish were all they could take out unless they wanted to go to jail. As they lugged those fish up the trail, Bobby suggested that Jared and Tim leave their rods and tackle home next time so they wouldn't have to pack all that dead weight. He immediately ducked, narrowly dodging the bullet of a slimy fish tail. The resulting cackle could have been heard down on main street Siletz.

Another time, in late summer, they had borrowed Uncle Ree's wooden scow that he had used as an illegal gillnetting boat many years before to fish the lower river for cutthroat trout. They liked to use wet flies, often catching and releasing dozens of fish before picking out a couple or three for dinner.

Bobby drew first cast while Jared rowed the boat and Tim drank beer. He side-casted a size 8 gray-colored Marabou muddler back under some overhanging willow bushes and dropped it into the dark shade of the green river water, let it sink a few inches, then stroked it in eight to ten inches at a time. On the second stroke, a six-pound trout hit that fly like a freight train. The giant fish could be seen in the depths flashing its silver side, then running hard, tugging on the line. Bobby held the fly rod nearly vertical, allowing the flexibility of the old Fenwick fiberglass rod to put a constant pressure on the cream-colored line and thereby keeping the hook in the sea-run cutthroat trout. After a prolonged battle, with Bobby showing all the fighting skills of a world class fly fisher, the trout was in the net and in the boat. None of the anglers could believe the size of the fish. The coloring was amazing with its orange-red throat markings that gave this magnificent fish the name "cutthroat." The black spots against a blue-green base color adorned the fish's back and tail. The belly of the fish was stark white against the blues, greens, and blazing orange.

None of the three boys had ever landed or even seen a cutthroat that would go over three pounds, and now this. They were all breathing hard, as though they had just run a race. This was by far the finest trout they had ever seen. They had fished that stretch of water for years and had never been graced with such a catch.

Without so much as a word, Bobby reached

down and slipped that beautiful fish out of the net and back into the water. "He was just too good for the pan," was his only comment.

They understood and never had a problem with the release of that magnificent trout. It had been, and still was, "just too good for the pan."

Uncle Ree had told them a story years before about a giant Chinook salmon he caught on opening day of the commercial net season. The great salmon had become tangled in Ree's net. It was at least a hundred pounds and probably more. Ree brought the fish aboard his boat and perused it with admiration. His partner went to club it and kill it but Ree wouldn't have it. He said, "This fish is just too good to go in some old tin can." At that he eased it back into the water and let it swim off. He always called it the "first fruits" fish, having turned it back to Creator.

Jared, Tim, and Bobby all remembered the story and now had their own "first fruits" fish to tell stories about.

10

Nobody to Mess With

Back in grade school Bobby had been heavy and received lots of teasing because of it. He never fought back. Most of the kids had come to think of him as a coward; Rez kids had to fight in order to attain the respect of their peers. There existed a pecking order based on fist-fighting ability. Bobby was at the very bottom of that order and everyone knew it. Consequently he had very few friends.

Jared had befriended him out of simple prox-imity, plus their moms were friends. Bobby and Jared spent countless hours playing with toy bull-dozers, trucks, and tractors in the big sandpile out back. They built little roads, parking lots, small mountains, and even airstrips. Sometimes Tim came and built roads with them; but his dad didn't like him "hanging around tribal housing" and seldom allowed him to hang out with Bobby and Jared except at school.

They all loved fishing together out at the bass pond. Bobby, of course, always caught the majority of the fish. Jared, who had the knack, cooked them up on sticks over a small campfire. All he ever added was salt, which he carried in a little shaker in his shirt pocket. Tim could eat more fish than Bobby and Jared put together and was proud of the fact.

When Bobby turned twelve he began to muscle up a little bit. It didn't really show because he was still fat. But Jared noticed it. One sunshiny day while Bobby and Jared were eating their sack lunches at one of the many picnic tables scattered around the school grounds, some of the tough kids came by to give them the usual hassle. Bobby, being a target of opportunity, was noticed right off.

Biron Nighthawk had been a bully all his life. He was big and loud, which Jared later learned was a bad combination. For whatever reason, Biron always homed in on Bobby rather than Jared. The hassle didn't usually amount to much, just some harsh words and the occasional push or shove; but lately it had begun to escalate into slaps and punches.

Biron slapped Bobby just for fun. Bobby allowed it as he always had. He ducked to cut the force of the slap but it connected anyway. Biron was cruel and knew how to inflict pain. He had learned well from his own father, who beat him and his mother on a regular basis. Bobby had his little black pup, Concho, with him that day and it cowered between his legs, piddling in fear. Concho was only twelve weeks old. He was a Labrador retriever with beautiful sad eyes. Bobby loved him, as did everyone who met the frisky pup.

Biron spotted little Concho and swiftly grabbed him by the tail and held him in the air, dancing a jig while the pup howled in fear and pain. Biron threw his head back and let out a war hoop, laughing while swinging Concho by the tail.

He caught a motion out of the corner of his eye just as Bobby tackled him. He was driven to the wet, rocky ground and before he could even yell, Bobby hit him in the face. He continued hitting him, driving his head into the gravel, bloodying his nose, cutting his lips, and blacking both eyes, until Biron finally lost consciousness. One of Biron's friends jumped Bobby from behind and was quickly elbowed in the teeth and then beaten to a bloody pulp. Jared, who had bloodied the nose of one of Biron's companions, could only watch as Bobby beat one after another, throwing them to the ground, kicking them and screaming like a banshee until they scattered like rats, helping each other limp off, leaving their blood trails behind.

Jared had never seen Bobby like that. He didn't know his friend was capable of standing up for himself that way. When they talked later, Bobby explained that he just couldn't stand seeing a little animal—or a little anything for that matter—abused. Biron and his friends never bothered Bobby or Jared again. In fact when Bobby and Jared showed up, they became scarce, slinking off into whatever shadow was available.

Bobby had fought like that only one other time. He was a sophomore in high school. His little sister had come home from school crying. She told him what the assistant soccer coach had done to her, how he had forced her to have sex with him. Bobby found him in the locker room putting gear away, and without so much as a word began to methodically punch him and kick him. He broke the man's bones, arms, legs, fingers, and nose. He picked him up and threw him headlong into the toilet, breaking the flush handle. As water spewed all over the floor, Bobby kicked the coach in the mouth, breaking several teeth. He then kicked him repeatedly in the groin. The agonizing screams were heard and the police were called.

After all was said and done, the soccer coach was arrested, tried, and incarcerated in the county jail for six months, most of which were spent in the hospital, followed by a year's probation.

Bobby spent two years in the McLaren School for Troubled Boys. He told Jared and Tim it was the easiest two years of his life because he was considered a hero there and didn't have to put up with his folks and their drunken parties. No one ever messed with Bobby after that.

Jared and Tim made Biron and his cronies' lives a living hell while Bobby was put away. Tim especially made it a point to pound the snot out of at least one of that crew every week or so, "just to keep myself in trim," he said.

11

A Girl with a Past

Sherri was twenty-one and single. She was, in her own words, "a girl with a past."

Her childhood had been safe, secure, and well sheltered. She attended Christian school. Her life had been structured, replete with all the expected activities. Her grades were outstanding. She graduated from high school with a 4.0 GPA and was accepted into Oregon State University, the University of Oregon, and Portland State University. She chose Portland State because of its strong literary program; and she did love literature. She hoped one day to teach it at the college level.

She had studied hard, taking in one new concept after another. Her faith in God was challenged, first by Darwin, then Buddha, then secular humanism. She was amazed at Marxism, intrigued by Leninism, and sickened by Nietzsche's writings. She regurgitated the teachings in essays and term papers. She prayed that her faith would remain strong. But it didn't.

She had dated very little in high school but had been astonished in her senior year to be elected prom queen. Vernon Lee, the captain of the football squad, asked her to prom. It was wonderful, almost an Alice-In-Wonderland experience. He danced well and even fetched her punch and cookies. They didn't hit it off in a romantic way but were good friends who had gone through school together since first grade. She enjoyed the evening and it was one of her treasured memories. In fact, that was probably her very most treasured memory from high school. She was one of the few members of her class who graduated as a virgin.

In college, it didn't take a beautiful girl like Sherri very long to hook up with the party crowd. She was short and blonde with a petite but full figure and the kind of eyes a guy could get lost in for a lifetime. Her grades began to slip as more and more of her time was spent in the company of the "in" crowd. She smoked pot, tried cocaine, and even played with some prescription drugs. She began consuming alcohol but didn't really acquire a taste for beer or hard liquor. She did like champagne and some of the sweeter wines, so she imbibed those when the party was on.

It was at one of the frat parties that she met Miles Jacobson. He was a senior and on the football squad. She noticed his striking blue eyes as soon as they were introduced. His red hair was cut short, like most of the jocks at PSU, and he was medium tall and muscular. He had laugh lines around his eyes.

"Hey, I've seen you around. Aren't you in the pep squad? I know I've seen you somewhere. How could a guy see someone like you and not remember where?" he asked while he sidled up to her at the party.

"You're Miles Jacobson, the football player!" She blushed and felt like an idiotic groupie. "Gawd, did I really say that?"

"Well, yeah, I was on the team, but the season's over now. Wanna get outa here with me? Some of the guys are gettin' together over at the Screamin' Irishman for some beers and pizza. Come on, it'll be fun. Sherri, right?"

At least he knows my name, she thought as she nodded assent. They left hand in hand.

His family had money and position in the Portland community. They owned income properties throughout Oregon and Washington and specialized in elderly care and assisted living centers.

It seemed to Sherri that his family had to have heart to take care of old folks.

They dated once or twice then began to see each other seriously. Miles had an apartment off campus and it wasn't long before Sherri was spending more time there than at the sorority house. She gave herself to him after the third date. Somehow it seemed like the right thing to do, so it had happened one evening after a wonderful dinner at the Olive Garden and a play at the campus theater. She hadn't planned it. She hadn't even considered it, but after a few glasses of champagne and some very sweet dancing in Miles' living room, it happened. Barry Manilow was crooning "I write the songs that make the whole world sing…" One thing led to another and the next thing she knew they were in his bed, exploring each other in every way. He didn't realize that she was a virgin—he was in too much of a fog from all the alcohol by then—and she chose not to tell him.

"… I write the songs that make the young girls cry …"

In the morning she and Miles went to breakfast at Denny's as though they were an old married couple. They made small talk. Sherri tried to define their relationship over ham and eggs but Miles was too elusive to get pinned down. The most she could get out of him was "Let's just give it some time and see how things go between us."

She hadn't even protected herself. She had never taken The Pill. She and her mother had never discussed it. Now she wished they had. She didn't carry condoms and apparently neither did Miles. She just wasn't prepared for the passion that had caused her to become so overwhelmed with raw emotion. They hadn't used a condom that first night nor did they the next three. She finally broke down and went to the walk-in clinic to get a prescription for The Pill. It was no problem, and she went back to the sorority house much more relaxed about the matter.

Sherri didn't hear from Miles for a few days. She tried calling but got no answer. She left messages; she even sent a note. No response. She didn't want to appear too anxious or too desperate or too anything, really. After all, she was still the same beautiful college student she'd been a week before.

She saw her as soon as she knocked and the door was opened. She was beautiful, brunette, and very tall, and she was wearing his bathrobe. Her hair was a mess, as was her lipstick. It was obvious what was going on.

Miles came to the door, wearing shorts, shouldering by the brunette. He was friendly but distant. "What's up?" he asked. Hadn't she realized that they were a casual couple with no real ties or commitment toward each other? Didn't she understand it was all part of the party scene, part of the fun? "Come on, Sherri, don't be so stupid, for God's sake!" Those were the last words she heard from him. "Jerk!"

Her heart was broken. She had thought they were falling in love. Well, speaking for herself, she had been. She stayed in bed at the sorority the next day and blubbered her way through two boxes of Kleenex. She felt used, like the worst kind of a fool. After she finished shedding all the tears, she bucked up and decided to go on with her life and "leave the selfish pig to his tall ugly brunette and his egocentric little excuse for a life."

She began attending classes in earnest with every intention of getting her grades back up where they belonged. Things started looking up. Her grades began to improve. She started feeling good about herself and the mistakes she had made. Her best bet was to move on and learn from her poor choices.

Seven weeks later she took a do-it-yourself pregnancy test and tested positive. She was paralyzed with fear. She didn't know what to do or who to turn to. After two more months of misery she finally called her mom, sobbing out the whole story over the phone. Her mom came and took her home to her old room. She often stared at the neon-colored images of the 1920s flappers on her girlhood wallpaper. That wallpaper had once helped her escape: fantasize about not being a "good girl." Now she was just the opposite, and it was real.

She felt dirty and unwanted, tainted by what she had done. She also felt stupid, used, and beyond naive. She considered suicide but wouldn't let herself dwell on that since she was carrying a child now. She had never agreed with suicide or euthanasia, but now she could see how some people could be so brokenhearted as to take a hard look at death, even end their life. She felt an empathy she had never known before. Maybe there was purpose in all of this pain. Perhaps it was time for this girl to grow up and become a woman.

On her first night back she cried so hard she feared it might hurt the baby. Then she knew she had to start thinking like a mother for the baby's sake. For the first time in years she prayed: "Lord, if you are there, please show me the way. I'm lost." She clutched her oldest teddy bear, still silky in some of its worn brown "fur"—one she'd had since she was a baby—and finally, fitfully, fell asleep.

12

Painful Memories

Sherri had been raised in a Protestant church and had learned the required things: the Ten Commandments, all sixty-six books of the Bible, the "key" scripture verses such as John 3:16, Second Timothy 1:7, and, of course, Psalm 23. She had memorized scripture and learned the proper doctrine. She successfully jumped through all those hoops in her childhood. She had even been baptized at her parents' insistence through full emersion in a 98-degree hot tub. Now *that* was commitment.

She had gone to Christian summer camp every summer since she was a little kid. Later she became one of the camp counselors, teaching Bible classes, leading field trips, and helping with the general oversight of a camp full of kids.

She was a teacher at vacation Bible school every spring at her church at home. Her contribution was teaching the first and second graders. She enjoyed reading stories to them about David and Goliath, Ruth and Naomi, and, of course, the life of Jesus, especially as a boy.

But none of that mattered much now. She hadn't understood who Jesus was until she had brought shame upon herself and her family. Sherri was brokenhearted over what she had done and what had become of her life. She had gone from a promising university scholar to a knocked-up dropout with hurt, angry, and disappointed parents, not to mention family and friends.

"Oh God! I'm the woman caught in adultery!" She remembered the story of the Pharisees dragging the scorned woman to Jesus and throwing her at His feet. They asked Him to judge her. Now His reply gave her hope: "Let him who is without sin cast the first stone." They dropped their rocks and left her with Jesus. He told her that He didn't condemn her but that she should move on and not commit adultery anymore. Yes, that story definitely gave her hope.

At her folks' church she knew she was barely tolerated. As her belly grew she could almost feel the wagging tongues of the congregants. Most didn't speak to her. Some, however, reached out to her, especially the more matronly among them. One little old lady named Bessy made it a point to always greet Sherri. She insisted that Sherri sit beside her; they sang the old hymns together, soprano and alto. Sherri's voice had always had a wonderful quality and she had sung in the alto section in the high school chorus.

Bessy told Sherri one day, "You know, dear, you're not the only young lady to find herself in the 'family way.' Some of these old snooties have had their problems too. I know. I've been in this church for forty years." Sherri almost laughed at Bessy's choice of words, as though they were still living in the 1800s. She felt lucky to have a friend like her even if she was decades older. Somehow, the decades didn't seem so long anymore.

Her parents bullied her into giving the baby up for adoption. Sherri had always been a pro-life proponent but had had second thoughts after having been exposed to all the different viewpoints discussed in college classes. She had begun to shift toward "women's rights," such as the right to choose what happened to their own bodies. The strong liberal message had begun to chip away at the beliefs she had held to for so long. Sherri had been leaning heavily toward abortion.

But her vote didn't seem to count for much when she came home pregnant. Her dad was firm in the position that she needed to have the baby, give it up for adoption, get strong again, and go back and finish her education. She would have more children when she had a husband and a career. End of story.

Sherri had acquiesced simply because she just didn't have the strength to fight any longer. Her mother did what she had always done; she sided with her husband.

The labor started late one cold and rainy night in November. Her mother was wonderful, helping her time the contractions and coaching her through the breathing exercises they had practiced together. The pain came in waves, with each wave becoming more intense. A call to the family doctor confirmed that this was the real thing, and off they went to the hospital.

Sherri didn't notice anything special about the hospital as she was wheeled into the delivery room except that everything looked white and smelled like alcohol. It brought back memories of getting shots as a child. She had never liked hospitals. She had definitely never enjoyed getting shots.

The delivery was long and pain filled, exhausting her beyond any weariness she had ever known. She breathed and pushed and breathed and pushed. She was dripping with perspiration.

It felt like the veins in her eyes might burst from the pressure of her labor. Her whole body was straining to deliver this child. She prayed for the strength to endure. It was beyond her ability to do this! Her mother held her hand while she followed the doctor's instructions. "Push now, Sherri! Push!"

"Breathe, Honey, breathe. That's it, keep breathing. Now push! There! Here it comes!"

After the baby came, she felt relief, then thankfulness that the pain was over. She got a glimpse of the newborn's hairless head as the nurse gently held it while the doctor tied and cut the umbilical cord. Then it was gone with not so much as a hello or a good-bye. She didn't even know if it was a boy or a girl. She had no doubt that the baby would be quickly passed off to the adoptive parents and whisked from the premises just in case she changed her mind.

She lay there empty, wondering what good she was to anyone now. She felt worthless, tired, and lifeless. Her mother gave her as much comfort as she could. Her father was conspicuously absent. She wept for herself and for her baby; whether boy or girl, she would have loved it.

She was moved from the delivery room to a quiet room at the end of the hall. Her mom left her a small stuffed puppy and some fuzzy slippers.

She tucked her in and fluffed the pillow, then bade her good night and whispered as she left, "Try to get some sleep now, Honey."

Sherri stared at the white ceiling tiles with little designs in them. One design leaped out at her; a tiny hand clutching a finger. She imagined her baby reaching out to her, touching her finger, then—gone. She couldn't look at the ceiling anymore. She rolled onto her side and looked at the green, lifeless floor and tried to empty her mind.

Her life was a sham now, without purpose or destiny. Her tears were cold on her cheeks as they ran down her face and melded with the stark white pillowcase. Mercifully, the good doctor gave her a strong sedative and she drifted off into a dreamless sleep. She had willed to herself that she would never dream again because she was afraid she would dream of the child who could have been hers, could have been theirs, the child who reached out to her.

13

A Special Place

Sherri moved to John and Linda's place just outside Siletz to get a break from her parents, especially her father, and figure out what she would do with the rest of her life. Returning to college was a possibility, perhaps next year. But right now she just needed some time to heal and think.

Uncle John, her mother's younger brother, was very patient with her, teaching her the basic chores of ranch life. She gathered eggs from the henhouse. Aunt Linda showed her how to slowly put her hand under the hen and gather the eggs.

There was a new litter of kittens in the barn. Sherri spent hours lying in the hay next to them, watching the mother cat taking care of them, licking them, inspecting them, and of course feeding them. She felt a maternal kinship to the cat and didn't fight the tears as they came coursing down her cheeks, falling freely into the hay mow. She instinctively knew that this was part of her healing process.

Uncle John and Aunt Linda had 120 acres of rich bottom land along the Siletz River. They raised cattle and hay and made just enough to pay the taxes on the property and a little extra if all went well. They both held down outside jobs, with Uncle John working at the hardware store and Aunt Linda working at the grocery store. Their beef cattle were sought after because they were grass fed and organic and brought good money from the locals who knew good beef when they ate it.

They invited her to stay as long as she wanted. They were kind and gentle with her, treating her as though she were their own daughter. She even attended church with them, mostly out of respect for them.

It was there, at the little Community Gospel church, that she dedicated her life to Jesus, not as a formal or public demonstration, but as a personal and heartfelt decision. She had a talk with Jesus, one on one, and through the tears of a broken heart she gave what was left of her life to Him. She realized that she had asked Jesus to serve her before. Now she wanted to serve Him. This was different.

The minister had been talking about what it means to "die to self" and let your past die with you. He told the story of his life, how he had dishonored himself and his family as a young man, how he had considered suicide. Then he shared how a man he had become friends with years before came to him, out of his past, in his darkest hour, and shared the truth about who Jesus really is. Somehow, miraculously, the truth took root in him and he prayed to Jesus Christ and gave his life to Him, even though he thought his life was over and worth nothing. He shared the pain and the triumph, the simple but powerful truth of how God took the shambles of his life and turned it into something beautiful, something "useful."

Sherri did something she never had. She came forward in front of everyone and cried like a newborn baby. She prayed with that minister and the ladies of the church who crowded around her, hugging her, holding her. The tears of healing flowed as she became cleansed by the Holy Hand of God. She felt herself being cared for in a loving, cleansing, gentle way.

She felt a weight lift from her. She knew something had happened, something powerful, something good and real beyond any reality she had previously known. She felt childlike and innocent. Sherri had never felt this way before. It was as though she were a totally new person.

Sherri's spiritual eyes were opened that day. Her hunger for the Bible became insatiable. She now had something she had never had or even knew existed. She was one with her Creator. Her old Bible, which had gathered dust for years, was now in constant use, the contents being absorbed into her spirit several times a day and even into the wee hours of the night.

Since that day, she prayed to the Lord in a personal way. She forgave those who had hurt her, abandoned her, used her, misled and betrayed her. She forgave and forgave and forgave. She didn't know she had so many tears in her body. She wept tears of joy, forgiveness, renewal, and healing. Then, finally, she forgave herself. That was the toughest part of all. But she had to let her old self go so the new Sherri could rise up and take her place of honor.

Sherri had had a born-again experience. She was now a new creation. The old Sherri was dead. The new Sherri had risen up like a phoenix. She no longer felt weak and pitiful. She was strong and getting stronger. She could breathe again. Her life was new, clean, and fresh. She came to the understanding that this life was not hers but her savior's.

"I love you, Jesus. Thank You so much. I want to serve You!"

14

Fighting with Cops

The Circle was a little bigger that evening with Tony Riggs and Sam Shaniko gracing the group. Tony was pretty beat-up looking. He later explained that the cops had worked him over with sticks when he had argued with a surly bartender and refused to leave the bar down on the Newport waterfront. The cops showed up and tried to talk him into leaving. He wouldn't, calling them "stinking pigs." They removed him physically, using their clubs and flashlights to defend themselves as Tony kicked and punched, trying to retain his freedom. It wasn't an unusual story at all and drew no comments from anyone in the group.

Jared thought back to the last time the cops had worked him over. He'd been drinking over at

Mickey's Pub when this big guy had bumped into him on the dance floor. The guy was pretty drunk and having a really good time dancing with this gal. It shouldn't have been a big deal—it hadn't been—but the guy was wearing a big white cowboy hat, a Stetson knockoff. Anyway, one thing led to another and the fists flew right there on the dance floor. Mickey's Pub always had a rule: "You fight outside and it's your business. In here and it's the cops' business."

They had shown up in record time. Jared was just finishing off the cowboy with a right cross when the next thing he knew, his ears were ringing and big black dots started dancing all around him. He swung blind once and connected with something or someone. As it turned out, he had connected with a city police officer, knocking him off his feet. There was no injury to the officer, other than to his pride, which turned out to be the worst thing Jared could have injured.

While "escorting" him to the county lockup, the police took a slight detour down to the "day use only" city park where they removed Jared from the squad car and taught him not to "sass his betters." His eyes were swollen shut for a week and his left hand was broken. Both kidneys were bruised and hurting inside. He pissed red for two weeks. It made setting chokers a real chore for the next couple of months but it was go to work or go hungry. Some lessons are hard learned.

"Yep, those nightsticks don't have a lot of give in 'em." He could still feel and hear the bones crunching when he had covered his face and his hand had been struck.

The eagle feather found its way into his hand again. He had been daydreaming, not getting a thing anyone said. He decided to pass it on then thought better of it. He, too, caressed the feather as he spoke:

"I got beat up by the cops once, actually a couple times. The last time I thought they was gonna kill me. I hurt like hell for a while after that. They just kept hittin' me, like I was a dog or somethin'. Funny thing. I never had any trouble with them unless I was drinkin'. Seems like I just piss 'em off sometimes. I really need to stay sober this time. It's been like forty-five days now and I'm startin' to feel okay again. I don't want to get beat up no more. That's all I have to say."

Shaniko nodded, understanding, as did Tony. Getting worked over was no new thing, especially when it came to the Newport cops. They were OK guys; they just got a gut full of Indians drinking and fighting in their town. It was an old problem, dating back to the 1850s when unscrupulous saloon keepers would sell liquor to the local Indians out the back door of the boardwalk bay-front saloons for two or three times the going rate. Illegal just meant that the price got higher, similar to Prohibition in the Roaring Twenties.

The eagle feather was passed to Tony. Head down, he spoke slowly while stroking it. "I tried the peyote church for a while. I kinda thought doin' the peyote and seekin' Creator might have some power in it. Seems like some of the guys been seekin' the 'old traditions' for a way to stay clean and sober. Most of 'em went back to usin'. The old ways are good and all, but the power ain't there no more, if it ever was. But, ya know, our people were never of the peyote ways anyway. So, it don't make no sense that we would copy the Piutes or the Choctaws or the Sioux or anybody for that matter. We were Rogue River Indians—well, my family is anyway. We didn't use no peyote or smoke out of the red rock pipes or any of that. I don't know. Confusing."

Tony continued: "Well, I been trying to quit drinkin' since forever. Lookin' at some prison time now so I'll prob'ly be out beatin' on the drum and doin' ceremonies with the brothers at Oregon State Pen before long. My 'court-appointed' says I can maybe make a deal, ya know, and only get a coupla' years this time. I dunno. Sick and tired of bein' sick and tired, ya know? Enit." He laughed a toothy laugh at his last comment, broke into a spastic coughing spell, and passed the eagle feather.

15

Bad News

Jared woke up to the clanging of the alarm clock and the sound of rain on the tinny aluminum roof of his trailer. Time to roll out for work. He made a lunch of bologna and cheese sandwiches, threw an apple and an orange into his lunch pail, and poured hot steaming coffee into his old beat-up thermos bottle. He was ready to go and took a minute or two to relax and sip his coffee. He heard the sound of tires on the gravel road just as the crummy rolled up and honked.

Jared crawled into the dark maw of the old crummy and sat down among the usual cacophony of snores and swishing windshield wipers. It was still windy and rainy; Jared knew this would be yet another day of cold and rain and mud, with some high southwest winds thrown in for good measure. *Thank God for good raingear,* he thought as he lit up a Marlboro and scratched himself. He wore black wool long johns today. His heavy wool mackinaw coat was a comfort in the cold weather.

Later that day, while Jared was up on Euchre Mountain setting chokers and enduring some of the nastiest weather of the season, Tony's dead body was found. It was on the Siletz riverbank, head and upper torso in the brown murky water, legs out on dry ground, with an empty bottle of Mad Dog 20/20 lying next to his muddy boots. The county coroner figured his body had been there since midnight. The Talking Circle had closed in prayer at ten or so. It had taken Tony less than two hours to drink himself into a drunken stupor and stagger to the riverbank. The county sheriff and the coroner looked the area over to determine whether or not they were dealing with a crime scene. The staggering footprints told a clear enough story. Tony had stumbled and staggered his way to the water's edge and passed out drunk. They both agreed that no crime had been committed, unless selling booze to a drunken Indian was considered criminal. The fact was that laws were already on the books concerning selling alcohol to an intoxicated person, Indian or otherwise.

The tired sheriff and the exhausted coroner adjourned to the Little Chief Cafe to talk it over some more and try to make some final determination as to what really happened. As it turned out, with just one set of tracks and no incriminating "smoking gun" evidence, it was just another Indian who drank too much and wandered down to the river to meet a bad end.

Tony's pants were unzipped. The officers speculated that he might have gone to the river to urinate, slipped or passed out, and the rest was history. At any rate, it was clear that however it went down, Tony had died alone. Drowning was deemed the official cause of death, with "extreme intoxication" a contributing factor.

16

Remembering

Jared heard the news as soon as he got into the crummy at the end of the day. One of the log truck drivers had brought word up to the landing crew, who passed it on to the rigging crew when they got into the crew bus. Everyone on the crew knew Tony. They stood around before loading up, at a loss for words, even words of comfort for one another. Jack was unusually silent even though he was a man of belief in the afterlife.

They didn't discuss Tony's death on the quiet ride down the hill, bumping along Euchre Creek and out onto the Kernville Highway. Jared remembered Tony's comments of the preceding night at the Circle. He seemed to have given up on himself and on life. He must've started drinking right after the Circle broke up and quickly had become drunk out of his mind.

Well, MD 20/20 would do that if a man had a notion, thought Jared. Fortified wines made for a quick, cheap drunk, as many a tribal member knew. He reflected back on the times when Tony had played football, a couple of years ahead of Jared, Tim, and Bobby. He had been one of the finest running backs the Coast League had ever seen. Jared envisioned Tony spinning and cutting with that crazy broken-field running style of his, slipping tackles, breaking some head-on, and just plain outfoxing others, then breaking into the open and outrunning everyone on the field. And when he made the end zone he had always let out a war hoop and danced around like a powwow dancer, strutting his stuff. He really looked happy when he did that and the crowd loved it too. He remembered the sound of the powwow drum pounding and the Siletz Warriors' yipping and ki-yiying every time a score was made.

Jared fought back tears and wondered if Tony had just got a gut full of his mess of a life. Prison was no place for Tony. He had a warrior's heart, even if he was a drunken ghost of what he had once been. Maybe that was the point. Tony must've gotten a glimpse of his future and had taken a different trail, the trail of death.

16: Remembering

"How lost did you feel?" Jared spoke to his friend who could no longer hear him. He wondered what he could have done for him. He had just left when Circle broke up, knowing his old friend was hurting. How selfish he felt. How powerless.

He saw his mother's eyes. They had been sad eyes but beautiful. She could say more with her eyes than most could with a hundred words. He remembered the way she had moved before she got sick. She walked softly, like a cat. She had strength, the enduring kind, but only to a point.

Jared found that he had become very accepting of death, be it sudden or long term, like what had happened to his mom. Death was such a part of life. The Siletz Tribe allowed its employees one day of funeral leave per month. To Jared that in itself was scary—and sometimes one day wasn't enough. Too many members were dying and it was driving Jared crazy. He wondered if it would ever change—could ever change. He desperately wanted a drink.

Uncle Ree stopped by that evening to see how Jared was doing. He came in, sat down, and drank coffee for a while, making small talk about hunting and fishing. Jared enjoyed the peace that seemed to follow the old gentleman around. He always felt better when in the company of Uncle Ree, a true tribal elder.

The following Saturday, Ree took Bobby and Jared up to the Valley of the Giants to spend some quiet time with the majestic old conifers. The wind blew a gentle symphony of healing as they sat quietly in the thick moss, backs leaning against the tree trunks. No verbal communication was necessary between the three tribal men as they basked in the glory of the sun filtering through millions of resin-rich, aromatic needles, spraying filtered light onto the forest floor. Their troubled souls healed quietly and slowly, together, as they mourned the tragic loss of their friend and tearfully celebrated the gift of his life.

17

Uncle Ree

Tyree Nelson Palmer was Jared's great uncle on his mother's side. Tyree got shortened to Ree when he was young. Nobody ever seemed to know why, but that's the nickname he was known by. Most everyone referred to him as "Uncle Ree" in later life.

He was born three generations removed from the Rogue River generation that had roamed their home country until the 1850s. His grandparents told him stories of the removal from their homeland. His great-grandmother gave birth to his grandmother on the trail up the coast. She stepped off the trail, gave birth while squatting under a red cedar, cleaned the baby, rested for a few minutes, then rejoined the column. Ree couldn't hear the story enough as a child and pestered Gramma for the story of how "her mom" had bore her, over and over.

She was small, weighing less than a hundred pounds. She stood under five feet. Her basketry was renowned in the community and was sought after, bringing a high price at the marketplace. She knew where the best clam beach was, how to gather mussels, and how to catch fish. She could tan hides using the brain from the animal. She could heal most wounds with her homemade salves of thistles, devils club (a club to fight off the devil with, as legend has it) and sheep grass. Her laugh could bring cheer to the hardest heart. Ree learned so much from her; yet he regretted not learning more.

When she died his heart was broken. He loved her more than life and went into mourning for more than a year. It was tradition to mourn for a full year when a loved one crossed over. Some clans wouldn't even mention the name of the departed while in mourning. Some never mentioned the name again until that name was given to a newborn baby. Ree was of that persuasion.

Ree longed to hear her laugh one more time; he remembered the pine casket being lowered into the black, loamy soil; he felt again the rain pelting him and the others as they shoveled the last of the dirt onto the mounded grave. He remembered the prayer he had spoken over her: "Creator, please care for this one in a special way. She had great vision. She loved us all; but mostly, she loved You. This, You know, since she is with You now."

Years later, when his parents were killed in a car crash, he repeated the process of mourning once more. A drunk driver had swerved into their lane, killing them instantly. Mom and Pop were in their late fifties at the time and should have had many good years left to them. He and Mary were both in shock. He particularly struggled with forgiveness issues for some time before finally giving the whole sordid mess over to Creator and asking Him to deal with it. Ree knew he just couldn't carry it himself any more. It was destroying him from the inside out.

Mary was very understanding and supportive of Ree throughout his mourning process. She consoled him, prayed for him, loved him as best she could in her own sweet way. She sustained him as only a loving spouse could do under such heartbreaking circumstances. Their love for each other grew deeper than ever before because this was one more test of their endurance, not only as human beings, but as a married couple. They became stronger together.

Ree was in his late twenties in 1954 when the Siletz Tribe was terminated. He didn't understand how the government, any government, especially the government that he had fought for in World War II, could tell a people that they were no longer a people. It was confusing. Many of the tribal people had been outraged that they had been given no say in this matter. They had only had the vote for thirty years or so, but they had embraced the right of citizenship and expected more dialogue from the government. Rumors of a "backroom deal" flew around the rez.

"Whadyamean we ain't a tribe no more?" he had asked his father. "What right does the president have to say we ain't a tribe no more?" His dad had no answer for him. He just looked at the ground in defeat and shook his old gray head.

Termination was sprung on them like a sharp-toothed bear trap. It took their identity. It took their land. Once again, it took their dignity. Ree told his great nephew Jared years later that it had been a time of confusion and fear among the people. He said that when times are like that, people are easily misled and taken advantage of. None of them had education or law degrees or any way to combat the injustice that befell them.

On a rare sunny day Uncle Ree once again took Jared and Bobby up into the deep woods of the Land Of The Giants. It was an amazing place.

Old growth fir and cedar were thick enough that the sky could hardly penetrate. Moss grew dense and lush as a carpet. Very little underbrush existed because there wasn't enough light under the great trees to support it.

The Land Of The Giants was a large tract of old growth fir, hemlock, and cedar that had been deeded to the United States Government and had been set aside so as not to be cut or logged.

They walked through the stand and were in awe of the overwhelming majesty of these mammoth trees. They were so tall that the tops couldn't be seen. They came out of the ground like behemoths, climbing into the cloudless sky. Their sheer bulk was nearly overwhelming to men and a tribute to Creator's powerful hand.

The average diameter of the trees was eight feet. Some of them were twelve, with a handful reaching to thirteen feet. It was dumbfounding to feast one's eyes upon these monarchs.

Uncle Ree told Jared and Bobby that he never tired of coming here. He said that he felt rejuvenated after every visit to this valley of life and awe. "This is where I come to visit the Creator. He is closer to me when I'm lying in the thick moss, looking up at the sky through these beautiful trees." Ree went on and on about the wonder of this stand of "tall and uncut" trees and of how they represented "what our people used to be, and could be again!"

It had taken them two hours by four-wheel drive to get to the Land Of The Giants and it had been worth every bouncing, pounding minute of it. The boys never forgot this sacred place and returned time and time again for solitude and rejuvenation. For Jared it became a good place to go and dream of things past and to come.

Uncle Ree explained to Jared and Bobby that at one time all the Oregon Coast had been covered by giants just like these. Mammoth spruce covered the lands closer to the ocean. They had been cut in World War II to supply timber for boats and airplanes. Much of it was wasted through high-grading the best cuts. Most of what was sawed down rotted on the ground, never to be harvested. It was a shame but was necessary in order to defeat the Axis powers that had chosen to make war against the United States and its allies.

He went on to explain that in 1855 the Siletz people had negotiated for a reservation that Congress had ratified; it had stretched for over a hundred miles north to south and extended inland to the top of the Coast Range. The tribe then owned 1.1 million acres of timbered land. The old growth timber on that land was prime in every way and

would still be standing today if it hadn't been stolen. He got a faraway look on his old leathery face
when he related how the land had been taken,
parcel after parcel, chunk after chunk, stand after
stand, by the government, without so much as a
how-do-you-do.

"Boys," he said, "if I live to be a hundred, and
I'm not lacking all that many years of making it, I
will never lose hope or lose heart that our people
will seek and find justice for all the thievery and
treachery and downright skullduggery that have
taken place against us. I believe the Creator is just
and invokes justice for His people."

He sat down in the cool shade on a buckskin log among the sword fern and the chantrelle
mushrooms and unashamedly wept. Neither Jared
nor Bobby had ever witnessed the old warrior shed
a tear before. Jared had watched in horror one day
when Uncle Ree had cut himself with a chain-
saw that kicked back. It cut a six-inch gash across
his thigh and gushed blood all over the place. Ree
never said a word or shed a tear over it. He just
bandaged it up with a dirty sweatshirt, got into his
old Ford pickup, and headed to town for stitches.
To see Ree weep now was confusing for the boys,
to say the least. Jared wondered if he would cry
when he was old. He hoped not. It was a pathetic
thing to see.

18

A Chetco Bride

ee married a dark-skinned girl named Mary. She was his high school sweetheart, a girl of the Chetco tribe. He met her one day while walking the old river trail. He was trying to catch a summer steelhead. She was picking blackberries and had stains on her mouth and hands from picking them and eating some of the juicier ones. He teased her about the stains on her teeth. She teased him back because he hadn't caught any fish. They walked home together, dated, fell in love, and were married after they graduated from high school.

His tribe was Shasta Costa. Their two tribes were, back before reservation days, separated by a major ridge that ran between two rivers. They both agreed that someday they would have children and when they did they would name them after their tribes. Ree thought Shasta was a great name for a girl or a boy—either one. Mary thought Chet was a great name for a boy and Chetco was a great name for a girl. They argued the matter good-naturedly. Nothing was ever settled for sure but they had fun bandying back and forth. It seemed they had fun no matter what they did as long as they did it together.

The two of them had twin sons who only lived a few days. The doctors didn't know what the tiny babies died of, but they called it "the consumption." Some folks later said that was a catchall diagnosis that could mean anything from pneumonia to cancer. As is tradition, they mourned their sons for a full year. They didn't dance at powwow; they stayed clear of most of the tribal gatherings and functions; Mary even went so far as to cut her long black hair. Ree missed her beautiful hair but understood her grief. Together, in private, Ree and Mary shared the pain of their children's passing.

When World War II came along, Ree joined the army; having completed their year of mourning, he left Mary to serve his country. He volunteered for the Army Rangers and saw enough action to last him a lifetime. His unit landed at Omaha Beach on D-Day. They fought their way up the beach, through machine gun fire, death, and destruction, clear to the outskirts of Berlin where they held an airstrip until Hitler's forces surrendered. They lost half their strength before they were relieved.

Some of the Rangers, Ree included, volunteered to be shipped to the Pacific Theatre and helped the U.S. and Allied forces take the blood-soaked beaches of Okinawa where they fought the Japanese up the slopes, cave by cave, crevice by crevice. They laid claim to that steep and rugged piece of real estate. The cost was dear; it was paid for in blood.

Ree told Jared that they all knew they would have been "in for one hell of a battle" if they had to invade mainland Japan. Their casualty projections were 50 to 75 percent in taking the beach-heads. When they heard that gigantic bombs had been dropped on Hiroshima and Nagasaki, they were glad that they had been given an alternative to invasion. Ree then said, "Nobody fights harder than someone fighting for his homeland. I'm sure I wouldn't be here today if those atom bombs hadn't been dropped—sad as that is."

He came home from the war with a Purple Heart, a Bronze Star for valor, and a missing pinkie finger. A grenade had gone off near him and taken the finger. He hadn't even noticed it because the fighting on the beachhead was so intense. He continued firing his BAR (Browning Automatic Rifle), successfully providing cover fire for a demolition crew who took out a fortified machine gun nest. He killed one enemy gunner outright, with a shot to the head, and wounded at least one more. The BAR was a highly effective tool for laying down a field of fire, and Ree was an excellent marksman with a cool head, having been a hunter from the time of his childhood.

He very nearly became a sniper since he was a crack shot. He ended up serving as the BAR man because he was able to handle the recoil and still hit his targets effectively. Some said the BAR kicked like a mule but that just never seemed to phase Ree. He was deadly accurate with it out to a thousand yards.

An hour after the battle was over a medic saw the bloody remnants of the finger and put a bandage on it. A week later a medical unit cleaned the wound, trimmed it up, and sewed up the stump. He was sent back to his unit and finished his tour until the war was over and he was rotated home. The only time the wound ever bothered him after that was when the weather got cold or when he bumped it. It also hurt like the dickens whenever he fired his hunting rifle, so he retired from hunting and became the camp cook and head bottle washer, which suited him just fine.

Ree never gave details about the things he had seen and done overseas. He never displayed his medals. He spoke in generalities, always trying to find some sort of a lesson in the war. He was a natural storyteller and loved to tell stories with Coyote, Wolf, Bear, and Cougar in them. He especially loved it when Rabbit and Squirrel ended up on the top of the heap. His stories were sought after by schoolkids and nieces and nephews. Ree and Mary never did have more children of their own, so it helped to have the neighborhood kids over and tell the stories. Mary always had cookies and cold milk for the little listeners. They loved Ree's storytelling and Mary's gentleness. Ree and Mary in turn loved the kids and the life and joy they brought into their home.

Mary had asked Ree about the war, about what it had been like. When he refused to talk about it, she pressed him, in the belief that it would be healing for him to let some of the horror out into the open. He looked at her and began to weep. He shook his big head and wept for the longest time. She held him then, not knowing what else to do, feeling guilty and helpless. He finally told her something she would hold dear for the rest of her life. "What I saw was so bad that I will never speak of it again. I will not speak the words that describe what I saw and felt. My mind has been damaged because of those images I have. If I could take a broom or a mop or a chain saw and get rid of them I would, but I can't. So when things got real bad, real scary, I thought of you. I saw your face when the blood was everywhere, when my friends were killed and maimed. I saw your face through the terror and the explosions of war. You saved me from going crazy, Mary girl, you saved me. Your love kept me from going off the deep end. When I was so scared I thought I might die, I saw your sweet eyes; I stroked your beautiful hair; I heard your little voice. Sometimes I held your letters against my heart."

She never asked him again; she just hugged him through the nightmares and the cold sweats that came in the darkness. She loved him for all her days, thankful that he had come home to her.

When Jared came along and then Tom left, Ree was a natural surrogate father. Great Uncle Ree became Jared's mentor, hunting partner, confidant, and friend—even though he was decades older. He saw to it that Jared knew the right ways to be a man, a warrior. Ree was a Christian and also a traditional Indian man. He loved to go to sweat lodge, powwow, and most of the ceremonies. He made and wore traditional regalia for those occasions. He stayed away from some of the ceremonies if they required taking part in ancestral worship or worship of anything besides Creator. But having made those small adjustments, he loved his tribe and their old ways, many of which had been lost on account of the reservation years.

Ree got frustrated when he couldn't find a piece of history he needed or a tradition or ceremony he wanted to know about. He was always searching archives at the library and listening to stories from the elders. He knew more tradition and history than most and that was a part of his frustration. He realized just how little he knew, how little was known by anyone in his tribe. He struggled with anger over what had been taken from them as a people; but as a Christian, one who forgives, he couldn't allow those frustrations to turn into grudges and hatred.

When Jared asked him about that issue, he replied, "Son, each of us has two wolves inside of us. The one wolf is evil and loves anger and hatred. The other loves goodness and serves at the Creator's bidding. These two wolves fight each other all the time." When Jared asked which wolf won, Ree replied, "Whichever wolf you feed the most will win the fight."

Jared never understood Ree's answer, but he respected the old man too much to doubt the truth of what he had said.

Upon returning from the war, Ree took a job with the State of Oregon. He was a heavy equipment operator and enjoyed it. He was given several chances to move into management and get off the machine but he turned them down every time. He had no desire to lead men after the things he had seen in the war. He was content to show up at seven a.m., work until four p.m., and take his hour off for lunch. He didn't want to write reports or give orders to anyone. He ran machines for thirty years, then retired and built a cabin on the Siletz River.

A year after they got the house built, Mary was diagnosed with breast cancer. She was at stage 3 and inoperable when it was discovered. She endured radiation and chemotherapy, which prolonged her life for another year. Ree cared for her at home, gently administering pain meds as needed and praying for her constantly. He loved her more every day in spite of the ravages of disease on her frail body. She slept more and more until one morning she crossed over. He was holding her hand when she quit breathing. Once again Ree went into mourning for a full year.

Jared was a real help to him during that year. He dragged him off on fishing and hunting trips and scouting trips in the off season. They even set a trapline that winter, which kept them both busy tending traps and caring for pelts. They caught beaver, bobcat, coyote, and otter. Since Mary's passing, Ree had more time to spend with Jared, which for Jared was a great blessing. Ree attended no gatherings or ceremonies, as was in keeping with mourning his wife, but Jared was with him more than ever and was a great comfort to the old man in his grief. Ree took long walks on the old river trail and prayed, asking Creator to care for his beloved Mary until Ree's time came to care for her himself. He was still in love with the pretty Chetco girl with berry stains on her mouth and hands. He always would be.

19

A Friend Named Tony

In their freshman year in high school Tony saved Jared's life. It was a clear Saturday in early fall. They had borrowed Uncle Ree's old Rogue River drift boat so they could chase steelhead in the Siletz River. Tony was an OK fisherman. He fished salmon roe most of the time. Occasionally he cast spoons—daredevils and steelies. They launched the boat at Moonshine Park and started downriver. It was a cool morning, not quite freezing but only missing it by a few degrees. Tony hooked and lost two good fish before they got one into the boat. Tony was by far the better oarsman of the two but Jared was no slouch at it. They both knew the river well enough to navigate it well. The drift boat handled white water with ease as long as it didn't hit a sharp rock and tear up the plywood bottom.

After they landed that first fish, Tony took the oars. They were shooting down through the "corner riffle" when Jared saw it: a tree had fallen into the river that night and no one else had seen it yet. Since Jared and Tony were the first ones down that day, they were "blessed" with the new discovery. The old spruce had finally given up the ghost and fallen out into the river, blocking the narrow passageway through the white water riffle. But they were committed to the run and couldn't get out of it; the rushing water was sucking them downstream at a dangerously fast clip.

Just as they hit the tree Jared stood up and tried to pull the boat over the partially submerged trunk. It was a long shot that didn't work. The boat flipped and was sucked under the tree. The sound of the boat breaking in two woke up campers in the park. "Did you hear that, Lottie? Down by the river; sounds like a wreck or something."

"Go back to sleep, Bert. They don't have car wrecks out in the river. I didn't hear a thing. You're having a bad dream."

Tony disappeared under the boat and was gone in the deep green of the dark, swirling water; Jared's feet went out from under him as the hull of the boat was sucked under the trunk of the old spruce tree. He felt the frigid water forced by the raging current into his mouth and nose as he was mercilessly dragged down by the undercurrent. His ears popped from the pressure of the water rushing into them. He desperately reached out and grabbed for a limb but was viciously torn from it by the raging water. He lost two fingernails in the futile attempt.

Being a strong swimmer, Jared began to regain some semblance of control and started to stroke up toward the surface. He could barely see in the swirling water below the downed spruce. It felt like his eyelids were being turned inside out and his lungs were bursting from holding his breath. He remembered starting for the surface when he felt a sharp pain as his forehead made contact with the shattered bow of the submerged boat, and then darkness overtook him. Strangely, he felt a peaceful bliss envelope him as though loving, gentle arms were rocking him to sleep. His body relaxed as he quit struggling and quietly sank to the bottom of the stream, bouncing along the gravel bottom, moving with the current into the shadows.

He came back to consciousness with Tony pounding on his chest and belly while yelling for him to wake up. It was, to say the least, a lousy way to wake up. He coughed and gagged for a while, lying there in the mud and gravel of the riverbank. After a few minutes he was able to take a breath without getting sick. He had thrown up bacon, eggs, and milky cheese. He wondered if he had broken some ribs.

Tony sat beside him, his head hung between his knees. He was mumbling something that Jared couldn't understand. When he asked him about it later, Tony told him he was thanking Great Spirit for sparing him. Jared replied, "You might want to pray that Uncle Ree spares us for wrecking his boat." He started to laugh, then gagged again and threw up.

As it turned out, Uncle Ree had laughed out loud. "I'm surprised that old boat lasted this long. I was gonna haul it to the dump a couple years ago, but you boys was havin' so much fun in it I just couldn't do it."

The boys had a good laugh over Uncle Ree's reaction to the loss of the boat. It was comforting to know that the old gentleman didn't care one iota about the drift boat. His only concern was for Jared and Tony.

Jared tried to thank Tony but his friend always changed the subject. He finally was allowed to give him a new steelhead rod and reel. That seemed to satisfy them both and the subject was laid to rest.

Tony had performed an almost impossible feat. He had dived deep into the treacherous waters of the riffle, grabbed Jared, and hauled him to shore.

He didn't use the classic lifeguard tow; he didn't know how. He just pulled him by the hair, yarded him up onto the gravel bar, and began pumping him out. He didn't have a clue how to resuscitate someone but "not knowing how" had never been a significant barrier to Tony. He got the job done. The proof was, Jared was alive and breathing, albeit sore and badly beaten up.

The boys survived the sinking but the old green Rogue River drift boat, or what was left of it, became a casualty of "the war on steelhead." Later, when a crew of loggers stopped with their chain saws and bucked off the spruce tree, the broken components of Ree's classic boat floated downstream to the next deep water and took up residence in the nooks and crannies of the river bottom. Passing steelhead fishermen commented for months, looking into the deep green and seeing the sunken remnants, until the winter floods came and cleansed the stream of man's debris, as it had done for all time.

After graduation Tony got a full ride to Oregon State University on a football scholarship but got drunk for a couple months that summer and never showed up for practice or for school. He just dropped off the radar and had pretty much stayed drunk ever since.

20

Death by the Numbers

Jared worked Monday through Friday without missing a day for two more months. He completed his ninety meetings in ninety days: Toledo NA meetings, Siletz AA meetings, and tribally sponsored talking circles and healing circles. One of the local churches even sponsored a healing circle he found interesting. They talked about the "Jesus Way," which seemed to have some power in it but was unpopular with the tribal community because the Christians had stolen so much land over the years. Another black mark against the Christians was the teaching that tribal regalia was a sin, as were drumming, smudging, singing, and powwow dancing. The tribal people just could not accept in their hearts that those things were not honoring to Creator. So, becoming a Jesus follower was a very hard thing. He did hear of a new church in town that taught that Jesus was in fact tribal and that dancing, drumming, and regalia were good ways to worship Creator. He thought he might check it out sometime. He doubted any Jesus church would teach such things but hoped that they would.

As his mind became stronger through continued sobriety, he was able to retain some of what Circle leaders had taught. He began to recognize death inside himself when he realized his people were some of the sickest people on the face of the earth. He picked up a few statistics from the Circle leaders. One of them was that Native women died at nine times the national average from alcoholism and cirrhosis of the liver.

Yep, his mom had been one of these; so had an aunt and a first cousin.

Another jarring fact was that Native American youth died from suicide at four times the national average.

Jared remembered all the times he had considered suicide just because he felt like such a screwup. One of his best friends, Robert, had committed suicide at the ripe old age of thirteen after his mom and dad were killed in a car wreck. His death was just one of many in Jared's circle of friends.

Another of his classmates, Anita, had killed

herself with sleeping pills after she accused her uncle of sexually molesting her but no one believed her—not even the cops. She had become an outcast in her family. Jared had always known Anita to be honest and straightforward. He couldn't help but wonder if the accusations she had made were true.

The Circle leader told them that Native American men are incarcerated at forty times the national average for crimes of homicide.

Jimmy-The-Fox's killer had been found, tried, convicted, and given twenty-five to life at the Oregon State Penitentiary. He was a Warm Springs Indian. Jared had friends on the rez who had served time for manslaughter, vehicular manslaughter, and murder in its varying degrees.

When they were told that the average age of death for Native American men is fifty-one, Jared began counting. He counted up eleven of his male relatives who had not lived even that long. Some had died in logging accidents. Some had died in auto accidents while drinking and driving. Some had died from disease. Influenza, chicken pox, diabetes, heart disease, and measles had all been killers in his family. One had been shot while resisting arrest.

But most of the deaths were alcohol related.

Jared came to realize that alcohol was a great killer of his people.

The statistic that really hit home was that the average age of death for Native American women was fifty-four. He didn't understand that. His mom had been only thirty-five when she died. Many, many of his aunts and their friends had died before fifty-four. Some had made it to sixty, but very few.

The statistic that 83 percent of Native Americans had been sexually abused was no surprise to Jared. He himself had been sexually abused by one of his mom's boyfriends and by an older girl cousin and her dad, his uncle. He knew his friends seldom talked about this sort of thing, but they lived in such crazy, drunken homes, with people coming and going at all hours, that he would have been surprised if sexual abuse were not a constant threat to them. This, in fact, had become a way of life in the village. He couldn't help but see Anita's face when the Circle leader was talking.

The Circle leader said something else that blew Jared away. "All this sickness is a result of 'historical trauma.'" He went on to define historical trauma as "the process of destroying all the authority, rules, rites, ways, belief systems, and structures, including family structures, of a civilization and thereby ripping the heart out of a people. The drugs, alcohol, and self-destructive behaviors are a symptom of that. Most people think it starts with drugs and alcohol. Not so; they come later."

Jared began to see a picture of himself. Was he dying inside and therefore outside? His thought process kicked into overdrive.

Jared realized that this historical trauma was key to what had happened to his people. *How could one undo historical trauma?* he asked himself. He couldn't. He realized that no man or government had the power to undo 160 years of historical trauma. That was how long it had lasted for his tribe. Some of the east coast tribes had endured five hundred years of it. It was bigger than him; it was bigger than all of them. They didn't have the power to overcome the evil wolf that man had created. The wolf had become too big. And now it fed on hatred and fear.

He understood then that the conquerors had taken away the rightful authority of the old chiefs. They could no longer oversee the tribes and clans. They could no longer take charge of the start of fishing, the end of the harvest, the hunting grounds, the burial sites. They no longer settled disputes or allowed or forbade marriages between the clans. The old chiefs had lost the right to protect their tribes, to pass on wisdom, to tell the history. They could no longer convey the ways of the people through traditional rites of passage, most of which had been lost forever.

The rules of the tribes had been lost. So many of them had been based on an intimate understanding of the ways of the land, the timing of the seasons, the movements of the fish and the animals. The slightest nuance in the atmosphere or the changing of a morning thermal breeze could instruct the old ones. To one who knew, the blossoming of a certain plant or the breakthrough of a type of mushroom could have great meaning for the people.

The rules of law had been lost: the rules of marriage and divorce and ownership and good manners. All of this and so much more had been forcibly ripped from his ancestors with not so much as a second thought.

The rites of passage that the young had gone through in order to assume their rightful place as men or women in the tribe had been taken. No wonder tribal people had so much trouble getting through life. To this day, they didn't know who they were and what was expected of them. No wonder drugs and alcohol were the "bad medicine" used to salve the pain of being lost in the modern world.

The ways of the people were gone too. The weaving of baskets had come back somewhat. But hunting and fishing skills were gone, as were the arts of canoe building and totem carving. The seasonal gathering times were gone. The marriage ceremonies (now only a choice between a white ceremony or shacking up), harvest ceremonies, and fishing ceremonies (where and when to start fishing—and when to stop) were gone. Jared knew the tribal culture department was trying to bring back some of the old ways; he was sure it would take much work and time.

The moving from village site to village site as the weather and seasons dictated was gone. So much, so many ways were gone forever.

The belief systems were so far gone that when he thought about it Jared could only tear up in frustration. No one really knew what the tribe's beliefs had been. In general, Creator, the Great Spirit, had been worshipped. But beyond that little was known of the deeper religious teachings of the Rogue River People. Many had guessed. Much had been surmised. Jared had read that a small portion of the old belief system had been researched through archives at the universities. The oldest of the elders passed a few things down but not many. Sadly enough, Jared knew that much of what the Siletz believed today had been borrowed from tribes like the Sioux, Cheyenne, and Crow. He knew that some beliefs had been borrowed from the Chinook tribes, who also suffered great historical trauma. Jared's Uncle Ree told him, "Our people did have a walk with the Creator once, but most of that was lost when we were put on the reservation. I think we were ready as a People to take the next step, which was to embrace His Son. But that was so twisted by the early settlers that it didn't take root." Jared thought that one over but it only confused him more. Sadly, as a whole, their beliefs were scattered. They certainly had no united vision.

The "New Age Movement" had attached itself to "Native Americanism" through false teachings by false gurus. Jared saw that his people were being used all over again by self-serving spiritualists.

Losing their cultural structures was probably the most damaging to the people. Jared wondered, who was in charge in the old days? What were the pecking orders? Who led this or that? What was the procedure for taking care of this, that, or the other? But far and away the most harmful had been the destruction of the family unit.

Jared remembered hearing about the government taking children away from parents and placing them in boarding schools. Uncle Ree had told him about how those children were mistreated at every level in those schools. They were sexually abused, culturally abused, and religiously and spiritually abused. He had said, "When those children came back to the reservation they had lost all ability to function within tribal society. Their hair had been cut short. They had 'learned' to dress in white man's clothes and they were not allowed to use their native language. Their identity had been taken from them. They were lost; so were their children and their grandchildren after them. They no longer knew how to raise children. The village and its holistic approach to raising children had been lost. Therefore the children were lost. Not one of them had any heart left. They didn't have anything to pass on except confusion. From that point on, the tribes were a sick and perverted people who turned to alcohol and drugs to 'medicate' their pain."

As Jared's brain cleared of the fog, he was beginning to see a pattern of death in his people, a plague of hopelessness. His heart was breaking at the suffering around him. He had thought that all cultures suffered from drugs and alcohol, from the fighting and lying, from the stealing and killing. He thought back on his mother, his aunties and uncles, his friends, the Tonys, the Jimmys, the Dorises, the Anitas, who had so much potential and so little result. He even thought of his dad. He felt the need to drink. Jared had a deep, empty pit in his life and couldn't seem to fill it. He knew he couldn't fix any of this. It was too big, too ugly, and too powerful. What could he do?

21

Hunting Bucks

Jared sat in the old creaking rocker sipping coffee one evening and thought back to the time when Tony, Bobby, Tim, Uncle Ree, and he had made their hunting camp back up in the Paradise Mountain country of upper Fall Creek. Paradise Mountain was noted for nice blacktail bucks. Tony had seen one with a twenty-inch rack in the spring of that year and had talked it up so much that they moved their camp from Euchre Mountain over to Paradise Mountain for that year's fall buck hunt. That was back in their "early" drinking days, before the booze really took hold.

"That old mossy-horn buck is the biggest thing I ever seen around these parts," exclaimed Tony for the hundredth time as they sat around the campfire sipping cold Bud. Uncle Ree drank coffee and didn't imbibe alcohol. He always cautioned the boys against it but never preached to them about it. He was respectful that way.

"I ain't never seen one that big! He's a good axe handle and a half across the ass end!" He went on to elaborate on the height, weight, color, and pure lightning-quick speed of this monster buck.

Rolling eyes accompanied by snoose-stained, toothy grins looked almost demonic in the flickering light of the pitch fire as the story unfolded. Tony's stories always grew as he imbibed further into the night. But the entertainment factor went up exponentially too as he gestured wildly about, waving his arms, bouncing up, jumping, and twisting—drawing on his old running back days, as though he were the big buck of the mountain on a dead run through a patch of windfalls, gliding through the tall and the uncut as only giant brush-bucks can do.

That had been four years ago. Tony had still been full of life: strong, quick, and athletic. The booze hadn't had a chance to take its full toll yet; it had only begun its deadly work.

Jared shook his head as if to shake away the cobwebs of painful memories. The way in which Tony's life had been wasted was painful for him. The beauty of the man consumed by the bottle, like so many others, was nothing less than fiendish theft, chemical murder.

They had hunted well that year. Tony had taken a nice three-point buck, dropping it cleanly from a distance of a hundred yards or so. It was done in the respectful way.

Uncle Ree had always tried to teach the young guys how to respect the animals they hunted: the deer had a spirit too and was to be held in high regard, never wasted nor hunted poorly. Quick kills were expected of the young hunters.

Jared, Tony, and the others listened and understood that Ree had heard these things from the old tribal elders who had, in turn, heard from their elders and so on. The teaching was sound but incomplete. So many of the old teachings had been lost, so much culture lost. But Ree always did the best he could. Tim, who was white, showed great respect for Uncle Ree when he taught them the good ways. In some ways, Tim was more Indian than some of the tribal members on the official rolls. He hunted well, fished well, and could sit quietly for hours without saying a word. He was also a good and trusted friend. Bobby took a quick shot at a very big, very quick buck, but missed. As great a fisherman as he was he made up for it with poor marksmanship. His .270 Winchester was one of the finest deer hunting calibers ever invented and his model 70 was a solid and accurate rifle topped with a Leupold VX 3 scope, but he just couldn't seem to pull it all together when there was a live animal involved. He didn't suffer from the Bambi syndrome—not a believer in killing animals; he just got "buck fever." His excitement level went off the charts with his heart pounding out of his chest so hard that he couldn't shoot or think straight. Most tribal hunters got over that when they were young and managed to put a kill or two under their belts, but not Bobby. He just kept shooting high or low or left or right. Sometimes he forgot to click off the safety. Once he tried to kill a large buck but couldn't see through the scope because his scope covers were still on. He dropped his rifle once because his hands were so sweaty.

Bobby received a lot of razzing over the years as a result of his buck fever. He always accepted it good-naturedly, teasing back when he could.

Jared took a very large bear early one morning. He had still-hunted into an old apple orchard on a good-sized bench back in the timber. The long-since abandoned homestead had an orchard of Yellow Delicious apple trees with a few red Gravensteins mixed in, twenty trees in all. The bears loved to come in at night and eat apples.

As Jared slipped into the grove of fruit trees

at daybreak with the thermal breeze in his face, he spied movement in one of the larger trees. He couldn't make out a clear form, but judging by the grunts, slurps, and general limb-breaking snaps he knew it had to be a bear. He slipped closer, taking care not to step on a limb or branch that would give him away. He stopped from time to time to check all around in case there were other critters he hadn't seen yet. He had learned that hard lesson as a young kid, having put his whole attention on a particular animal and snuck toward it only to jump another animal almost at his feet because he had been concentrating on the original one.

The wind swirled just a little, but that's all it took. The bear grunted, then dropped to the ground facing Jared, not really seeing him since the hunter had frozen in place. It was a large male, well over four hundred pounds. It swung its head from side to side as it stood on its hind legs sniffing the wind; its powerful sense of smell was its primary defense mechanism as well as its main tool for finding food.

Jared was less than fifty feet from the big male when he slowly began to raise the old .35 Marlin lever-action rifle. He squeezed the trigger slightly so as to eliminate the clicking sound when the hammer was thumbed back to full cock. He eased his thumb off the hammer and began to slowly squeeze the trigger as the front bead settled on a white spot on the bear's powerful upper chest.

Just as he squeezed off the shot, the bear swung to one side, pivoting on its massive hind legs. The bullet grazed it, cutting hair, as the two-hundred-grain bullet burned a path on the bear's muscular shoulder, leaving only a painful flesh wound. Without hesitation the enraged bear changed course and charged Jared, covering ground at an impossible rate of speed. Jared levered a fresh cartridge into the chamber and instinctively fired again, this time driving the bullet into the bruin's powerful chest, knocking it down with authority. The bear went down but was up immediately, bawling its adrenalin-fueled rage at this puny man who had inflicted such horrible pain upon him. Saliva and blood spewed from his clacking jaws as he tore toward Jared once more. This time the crazed animal got to within ten feet of the young hunter before the next bullet broke his neck, downing him once and for all.

Was it his imagination or had some level of understanding passed over the animal's face as the rifle bucked in Jared's sweating hands, nudging his shoulder with the recoil? The smoke obscured his vision for a fraction of a second as he watched the majestic black monarch kick his last. He died in a pool of bright red frothy blood contrasting against thick green orchard grass.

Jared slept well and deep that night in the old canvas wall tent. Having told his story over and over again around the fire, he had removed layer after layer of fear. It was as though the telling somehow freed him from the fear of having nearly been killed by those teeth and claws. He was true to the old bear and their story as he mentioned the look that passed over the bear's features just before death took him. He felt a strange kinship to the animal he had killed, as though they had shared a spiritual moment together.

Uncle Ree seemed to understand what had happened. He didn't elaborate in the least, but he seemed to have a kind of insight into what had taken place. Tim understood too. Bobby never had a clue.

They were awakened to the sound of Uncle Ree bragging about his camp coffee and how it not only tasted good but could wake the dead if administered quickly and abundantly. "Abundant" was one of his favorite words. He had learned it from a Pentecostal preacher years before and was partial to its meaning and use.

"Rise and shine! Come and get it, boys. It's hot, it's good, and in abundant measure, even if I do have to brag on it myself," hollered old Ree.

Jared had lain in his sleeping bag as long as he

could but couldn't resist the smell of frying bacon and Uncle Ree's cattle call to come and get some grub.

That hunt now seemed like it had happened a long, long time ago. It was the last good time he could remember with Tony. After that he just seemed to go off into another world; they all did except for Ree, who stood on the sidelines like a parent or a coach waiting for the team to come off the field after the game, occasionally shouting encouragement and instruction onto the field but from a foggy distance.

22

Sunshine on the Mountain

It was the month of May and Euchre Mountain was in the final throes of yet another wet winter; technically it was spring. It had snowed in January. The snow had washed away in a torrential rainstorm in March, flooding the creeks and rivers to the point of overflowing their banks. A handful of houses had washed down the mud-brown Siletz River along with cows, horses, root wads, logs, miscellaneous flotsam, picnic tables, and runaway boats. But it wasn't any worse than a half dozen other run-off years in the last couple of decades.

April had endured one rain and windstorm after another, causing misery upon misery for the tired rigging crew as they moved wood off the hillside, day after dark, gloomy day.

Finally the annual miracle arrived; the sun came out, bringing with it the warmth required to recover from the long winter. The songbirds came back along with the ducks and the geese honking and whistling overhead on their annual northbound migration.

The whales came back, magnetically slow-swimming their way north to the calving grounds in the Arctic, the Bering Sea, and the Gulf of Alaska.

The deer and elk slipped out into the openings to replenish the lost flesh on their sinewed bones, their numbers and their weight depleted by poor diet, cold weather, and predation. The green cowslip, orchard grass, and clover were consumed as the earth brought them forth. Even the salmonberry stalks were "greening up" and filling with protein. It was time for the winter-lean herbivores to eat, prosper, and propagate their species.

Bears that had been in winter sleep in dens under old-growth stumps made an appearance in search of the spring grasses and browse on the south-facing, sun-enriched, higher elevation slopes. They especially sought the cambium-rich inner bark of Douglas fir trees, much to the chagrin of the timber companies.

Bobcats, coyotes, and cougars all made their nocturnal rounds in search of emaciated animals to cull from the herds. They sought deer fawns and elk calves that would make ultra-nutritious meals for their upcoming spring litters.

The green-up lifted the spirits of the tired loggers as they went about their day-to-day work down in the log-filled canyons. Often twenty-five-hundred feet down, setting their chokers, rigging their lines and machines, these men moved tons of wood fiber in the form of tree-length logs from the hillsides and creek bottoms to the tops of ridges and onto landings. The logs were processed and hauled by log trucks down the winding, steep, narrow roads into town.

Maligned as the lackeys of timber barons, these underpaid loggers worked from daylight to near darkness, in all weather conditions, drawing their wages and contributing to a fragile economy, not really knowing whether the logging industry was good or bad; they simply did what they could to survive in a world of utility bills, car payments, rent, school clothes, and a myriad of financial pressures that didn't care how the men earned their money, as long as they did.

They lived in a world of bruised legs, scratched arms, and aching backs, where the hardship of "cruel hard labor" was an everyday reality. They performed their daily tasks on steep, brushy slopes where most people would have better sense than to try to walk; and they did it while carrying tools that could sometimes weigh in excess of a hundred pounds.

There is nothing heroic about it. No medals are given to men who work in mud, snow, wind, and rain. No awards exist that recognize the discomfort of steep ground, slick footing, and dangerous conditions. No recognition is given to one who struggles to set a stiff choker around a tight brush-choked log while the weather is spitting sleet and snow in a screaming gale.

An old weatherworn hook-tender said it best. "We don't cut and log old growth timber anymore. We log little second and third growth, pint-sized trees, so ordinary folks like us can have paper towels and toilet paper, so kids can have something to write on and newspapers can print the news. Lawyers print up eviction notices; banks write repossession papers. Hell, we might even be part of ol' Will Shakespeare being printed up, or the Bible. Who really knows?"

His simple words encapsulate a reality for today's working logger, many of whom are tribal; there is no glory in sending small logs to a technologically wondrous pulp mill in Toledo, Oregon. There is just a living to be made, and just barely that.

But paper is a necessary commodity in today's

world. It is the lifeblood of "hard" communication, found in every office, school, factory, airplane, military organization, and home in America and throughout the world; it is everywhere and used for virtually everything.

The spring sun had come out and dried the hillside for the first time in months. The rigging crew was feeling pretty frisky and moving wood at a good clip. It looked like they might plug the landing, there was such a volume of wood going in. If they did plug the landing they usually got a fifteen- or twenty- minute break while the landing crew caught up on processing and stacking and sorting the logs.

Brad was sending the signals plenty early, barely giving Franky, Jack, and Jared time to get into the clear before the turn left its bed and was hoisted to the carriage, then gone. But they were enjoying the game, moving with alacrity from log to log at a dead run. Not too many crews had the ability to move this volume of wood. They took pride in the fact that they could.

Click, click, click. The three choker bells clicked shut, locking them to their respective logs. Brad blew the whistle and the crew scrambled to get clear. Jared made it to the knob where Brad was and into the clear. Franky was next, then Jack. But as Jack started up the last log, his foot hung up on a root. Brad yelled to "run or die," laughing as he said it.

They hadn't noticed how rotten the old snag was when it was standing next to the sky-line. As the drop line came tight it slapped into the side of the snag and the top broke out of it. It flew through the air toward the rigging crew as if in slow motion, tumbling end over end. It struck Jack squarely in the back, making a sound like the cracking of an eggshell. He never knew what hit him.

Brad's laugh turned to a sob as he witnessed, as in slow motion, the snag slamming into Jack, killing him.

They all yelled, "Jack, look out!" But it was too late. The broken snag top had come like a bullet. Nothing short of a miracle could have stopped it.

Had he made it even ten more feet he would have been in the clear. A fluke? Yes and no. The sad truth was, he was just too close. They had all been too close. Things happened so fast. His neck was broken, as was his back. The piece of snag that hit Jack was doing over a hundred miles an hour and weighed more than a thousand pounds. He never stood a chance.

Jared was amazed at how quickly a man's life could be snuffed out. One moment Jack was there running up that log, then his foot hung up for a second, then he was dead. No moans, no crying out. He was dead, gone, lifeless.

They screamed "No! No! No!" but to no avail. They moaned as harsh reality struck home. Franky fell to his knees, dry-heaving.

Brad blew seven long whistles to inform everyone that someone was badly injured. In minutes other crew members, supervisors, bosses, and the owner of the company were on the site. Officials were called. The county sheriff was informed that a death had taken place. He in turn called the coroner. A life-flight helicopter appeared on the horizon and began circling, looking for the site, the rotor blades whop-whopping as it hovered, then landed on the ridge.

All those gathered around the body tried to console Brad, Franky, and Jared. Brad stood as if in a dream, staring out toward the standing timber. Franky was sitting on a stump crying and moaning. Jared was silent, staring at the paramedics as they ministered to Jack's dead body, delivering shocks with the AED and giving CPR. Nothing helped. Their best efforts couldn't bring him back to life.

Solemnly they waited for the coroner to come out and make his examination. Jack was pronounced dead and put on a basket stretcher. His body was covered with sweatshirts to keep the dirt off. Franky, Brad, Jared, a deputy sheriff, and two paramedics picked him up and carried him to the landing where a hearse was waiting. They packed him as though in a daze. No words were exchanged. They gently placed his earthly remains into the back of the hearse, then turned away and walked over to the county sheriff's black SUV.

They answered the questions that were asked. It was all very formal, quiet, and surreal, as though they were somewhere else, watching things from another place, peering through fog. They never mentioned the run-or-die game they had been playing. They became co-conspirators in the cover-up. They lied like dogs.

Each of them secretly wondered whether Jack's relationship with Jesus had been working for or against him. Since none of them believed the stuff he preached, it remained a mystery. There may or may not have been a service for Jack; Jared didn't know. He wouldn't have gone even had he known because it would just be to comfort the family anyway. Nothing really meant anything anymore.

Jared was ready for a change. He was desperate for it. His mind and his heart required it. His very soul was dying. Jack's loss only made things worse. He worked for the outfit for another week. It was a long and dark week.

He knew he needed a change of everything:

scenery, company, activities—everything. He wasn't a praying guy at all, but he whispered a silent prayer to the Creator as he finished setting the last choker for the day. The quitting whistle blew and he started the long steep, brush-choked climb up to the landing. "Creator, if you are there, I need a change. Please help me."

He gave Tom, the siderod, his notice that night. "I'm pullin' out. Done until at least next fall. When can I pick up my check?" The old siderod gave him a knowing look and nodded.

He was informed that he could pick up his pay on Monday afternoon.

"Sorry to lose you, Jare. You shaped up real good in the last coupla months. Good luck. Hope to see ya next fall. There'll be plenty'a work when you're ready," replied the old weather-worn boss, slapping Jared on the back as he headed for the crummy and the long ride down the mountain. Since this was Friday night, Jared would have the weekend to get ready to travel. He already knew he was headed south, to the Rogue River country. He had been drawn that way for some time now and he needed to go.

His people, the Shasta Costas, had lived on the Rogue River in the old days, back in the 1800s and for thousands of years before that. He felt deeply in his soul that if he were to have any healing it would take place in the waters of the Rogue. He dreamed of soaking in the cool tribal waters late into the night. He daydreamed of hiking the river trails, taking in the aromas of the giant pine, cedar, and oak trees. He ached to bask in the glory of the great stands of old-growth fir. The rugged slopes called to him. The steep gullies leading up to dark-timbered headwalls spoke his name. Somehow he knew in his heart that he must go home. His sanity required it. His very life depended on it.

23

A Pleasant Surprise

Jared's old pickup was nothing to brag about, a 1972 Ford half ton, dark blue with a white canopy. He had always wanted a red truck but was proud of his blue "rez truck," replete with rust and dents. It had come along as a really good buy right after payday a while back. He liked the 360 V-8, the four-speed tranny, and the fact that it was a four-wheel drive. The tires were pretty good, nothing fancy, just plain-jane mud and snow grips. He liked them because they were dependable in the mud and held up good on all types of roads: pavement, gravel, or mud. The rig wasn't much too look at but Jared knew he could trust the old steed.

He loaded it up with the essentials he would need to camp for a while. A ten-foot dome tent, another bargain, had served him well in most kinds of mild weather. It held up to rain and even light snow, was big enough to hold his sleeping bag and little gas cookstove, cast iron pots, dutch oven, and some limited comfort supplies such as shaving gear and personal belongings.

Jared kept most of his stuff in the pickup when camping because it was easier that way and the canopy kept things nice and dry. His food—canned venison, potatoes, and corn—stayed fine in the rig. He kept his rifle, bow, arrows, ammunition, fishing gear, binoculars, and camera inside the cab where he could lock them up for security purposes.

He had been off probation for a few months now and was able to hunt and fish and carry his rifle and pistol legally. He owned a nice .300 Winchester Magnum as well as his old .35 bear rifle. He kept them both in canvas scabbards behind the seat. It was legal as long as they were both unloaded and zipped into the scabbards.

Jared was meticulous about the preparation of his fishing gear since the Rogue and other local tributaries held trout, steelhead, and salmon in some abundance. He was partial to pan-fried trout so he made sure to lay up a good number of wet and dry flies for the fly rod.

He also put a good steelhead rod on board;

he'd rig it for bait fishing for steelhead and salmon as those opportunities and river conditions presented themselves.

He always took a light backpack that held the essentials for long hikes and spike camps. He usually included things like waterproof matches and some sliced Douglas fir pitch for starting fires— rain or shine. A small plastic tarp, a space blanket, and extra .22 ammunition for the revolver were important to add to his pack. A handful of flies and fishing line for rigging willow poles for creek fishing; a couple bread sacks for gathering mushrooms and wild onions; flashlight and batteries; a mirror, wool sock hat, tin cup, and salt were essential. He added whatever grub he might need for snacks and "just-in-case food." The last consisted of a pouch or two of freeze-dried food and a few candy bars. Snickers were his all-time favorite. Hershey's with almonds were a close second. The whole pack weighed less than ten pounds and was handy to have. He had lived out of that pack more than once while hiking in the backcountry.

He oftentimes supplemented his food with ruffed and blue grouse and the occasional cottontail rabbit or porcupine. These could be cooked over an open fire with ease. As with most wild game, large or small, flavoring with salt was the key to a delicious meal as opposed to a bland one.

Jared remembered the words of Crocodile Dundee: "You can live on it, but it tastes like shit."

Jared thought Dundee had a good point but should have shown more respect for the animal whose life he had taken and whose flesh he was eating. Jared thought he was beginning to sound like Uncle Ree. Maybe the "good wolf" was starting to speak up.

He changed the oil and filter in the pickup, checked the water for antifreeze, checked the tranny and the rear ends, and greased every zerk fitting he could find. He even went so far as to check the air pressure in the tires, putting forty-two pounds in each.

His tire chains were on board as were a single-bitted axe, a shovel, and a good spare tire with jack and star wrench. He put in two five-gallon cans, one for extra gas and the other for fresh water. He had a couple of extra quarts of oil after the oil change and stashed them in the toolbox along with his rain gear and extra tools.

Jared asked Bobby to hang out at his place as much as possible. The rent was paid up for a couple of months so that wouldn't be a problem. Since his phone didn't work he didn't have a bill to pay. The lights would be fine since he usually didn't pay until into the third month anyway and planned to be back by then. Jared wondered if Bobby would lose some weight since Jared wouldn't be there to cook for him.

He knew his trailer would be targeted for burglary unless Bobby stayed close. Bobby was no dummy; he would keep things safe.

Jared pulled up at the office in the loaded pickup, grabbed his check, went over to the bank and cashed it, topped off the fuel tank, and left town with $673.44 in his wallet and a crisp $100 bill hidden in the toolbox. Hopefully this would be more than enough to hang out for a frugal month or two on the Rogue.

He swung by Country Market for a cold pop and a pepperoni stick. As he went to the counter to pay, he noticed her. She was waiting on a customer at the other cash register, laughing and talking, her voice as sweet as warm honey. He changed to the other line so she could wait on him.

When their eyes met he felt something, something he had never felt before. He seemed to inhale the air differently, in a better and deeper way. She smiled at him and asked a question. She asked again, then looked quizzically at him as though to see if he were awake, asleep, or perhaps drunk.

"Paper or plastic, sir?"

God, she's beautiful, he almost said aloud.

"Paper, please. I might need it for starting fires."

"Do you start a lot of fires?" she asked with a twinkle in her eye.

"Uh, no, I mean, I'm going on a camping trip. It, the paper, might come in handy for starting campfires. Besides, I work in the woods and I support the industry as best I can."

He felt inadequate as she looked him in the eye and laughed. He didn't remember seeing her before. Her eyes were green and hazel, hard to describe. She was sort of blonde but not flashy. He couldn't take his eyes off her, even when she gave him his change and raised her eyebrows. He took the hint.

"I'm Jared." He held out his hand.

She took it and replied, "I'm glad to meet you, Jared. I'm Sherri."

As he left the store he wondered if she had felt something too. Or was he just being silly? Wasn't he a little old for puppy love? He knew that love at first sight was only a dream found in books and Disney movies. Yet he had felt something new, something wonderful.

"Hey, Jared."

He turned to see her standing just outside the door, leaning against a wall that had turned into a cluttered community bulletin board.

"I'm going on break. I have time for coffee if you do."

He nodded an affirmation and followed her to the back of the store where the employee coffee pot was kept alongside a picnic table. They poured coffee into Styrofoam cups and sat down across from each other, neither taking the initiative to talk. Finally Sherri spoke.

"I'm feeling kinda funny asking you to coffee like that. I'm really shy most of the time. You must think I'm really forward, or desperate, or something."

He hadn't given it a thought. He was just rejoicing in his heart that this cute little gal would even notice him, let alone ask him to coffee.

"Fact is, I'm the shy one. If I could'a said it I would'a asked you for coffee. I've always been really shy around girls. But I'm glad you asked 'cause, well, I like coffee."

They both burst out laughing. They felt the attraction and saw the humor in what he had just said. Her eyes danced at him. His danced back.

He hung around town until she got off work. She told him she had grown up in the Corvallis area, where her dad was a construction foreman and her mom a homemaker and substitute teacher.

Sherri had been raised as a church girl, sang in

the choir, took part in youth group activities, and had read her Bible cover to cover. She referred to herself as "nonreligious—but in love with Jesus."

She talked about college, just hitting the high spots. He talked about logging, again just hitting the high spots.

Jared never claimed to understand half of what she said but he enjoyed listening to her as they got to know each other sitting together in his old pickup, sipping grape pop and sharing stories about themselves, their families, and friends.

He told her about his family, hunting, fishing, and gatherings; he even spilled about all the drinking problems, the drugs, the jail time—including his own. He shared the fact that he struggled with nightmares, most of which he didn't understand.

She listened with intensity, not judging him, but understanding to the best of her ability. They talked for hours, getting to know each other, sharing things they had never shared before with anyone. They didn't even hold hands.

Sherri asked, "You're tribal, right? It's funny. A lot of the people around here are part of the tribe, but they don't all look like it. So … how much Indian blood do you have, Jared?"

Jared, sighing, replied, "Yeah, I'm tribal."

With a little frown he said, "Hey, how do I say this? But, well, you need to know this. It's not right to ask someone how much Indian they are. It really upsets some of the members. The reason is 'cause the BIA and Indian agents and others used to use the blood quantum percentage against certain families, ya know … when it came to paying out lease payments or distributing food and stuff. So, just so you know, it's not cool to ask that."

"Wow, I didn't know that. How do you learn all this stuff? I mean, the history books never taught any of this. I don't even know what the 'real' history is. How did you find out this stuff?" asked Sherri.

"Yeah, the history we had in school talked about Squanto and Captain Smith and all those guys like they were big heroes or something. The stories I heard as a kid from the elders didn't sound like that at all," Jared said. "Most of it's not pretty … the soldiers on horseback with rifles across the pommels of their saddles, herding a hundred warriors with their hands tied together and tethered to a long rope stretching for three hundred feet, moving north on the sandy trail in the cold rain … Yeah, the stories bring tears to your eyes if you can stand to listen."

Sherri changed the subject and asked, "So you just need some time off work? Are you burnt out?"

"Sorta. Well, it's more than that. You hear about the logger got killed last week up on Euchre? He was a friend of mine, name of Jack—he worked on my crew. Anyway, I gotta get my head on straight."

"I'm sorry, Jared. I just didn't think. Yes, I did hear about a logging accident. It was all over town. It must've been hard for you, losing your friend so suddenly."

"It was. It was more than hard. Jack was about the most special guy I've ever known. But, ya know, I never told him that. Anyway, I been thinkin' about goin' on Vision Quest for a while now. I think it's time. I'm pretty sure he would understand."

"What is a vision quest?" Sherri asked.

"Sorry to correct you again, but it's 'Vision Quest.' It means to go to a sacred place and seek out Creator and maybe be given a vision, like a life-vision. Vision Quest is like a sacrament, a thing young men do when they start gettin' serious about life. And sometimes Creator gives you a new name." His face reddened at his last comment.

"I'm trying to understand. And I'm glad you're taking life more seriously now."

"Well, I don't even know if I believe in Creator; but the second step in the Big Book, you know, the Alcoholics Anonymous Book, says I need to 'acknowledge a being greater than myself who can restore my sanity.' This has been burnin' in me for some time. Anyway, I need to go try. My sanity isn't what it ought to be." He made a half-hearted smirk.

He realized that they had sat talking in his pickup all night as the dawn began to brighten the cobalt-blue eastern sky; he told her he needed to be leaving and described in general terms where he would be. He was surprised when she didn't think he was crazy. He was further amazed at what she said next.

"I have tried to walk with the Holy Spirit since I was a little kid. Lately I have just begun to learn how. I think your people call Him the 'Great Spirit.' Anyway, He is the one who told me to follow you out of the store and invite you to coffee. I guess I should've told you that right off. Anyway, I'm glad He did—really glad.

"Jared, I believe that the Great Spirit heals people in different ways. Sometimes it's with miracles. Sometimes it's a process. Sometimes He uses people: doctors, therapists, counselors, and ministers. But it looks to me like God is sending you on a vision quest, I mean, on Vision Quest, to find Him. I think He's going to heal you from this alcohol sickness and from all the other sickness in your life. He has a plan for you, Jared."

Sherri blushed at her last words. She wondered if she had said too much.

Jared hadn't seen a girl blush in years, at least not a grown woman like Sherri. He found it refreshing somehow, as though sweetness and innocence still existed here on the rez. He remembered his mom blushing at times. It was a very sweet memory. In thinking back, he could remember how the "traditional women" dancers at powwow carried themselves, very dignified. He had always respected them. But so many of the "rez" girls had no code of conduct; neither did the boys for that matter. For the most part, they just seemed to follow their desires.

He dropped Sherri off at her car, still parked in back of the store, said a quiet good-bye, and promised to look her up when he got back into town.

"Wait a minute." She ran to her car, spent a few moments on something, then ran back. She handed him a paper sack. "Just a little gift" she said. Then she turned and walked to her car, a pale green Volkswagen bug. She waved as she started it up and putted out onto the street, leaving a thin vapor of blue smoke behind her.

24

Heading South

Jared drove south on Highway 101, the Coast Highway, enjoying the minimal springtime traffic and the view of the Pacific and her long white beaches. The sun was out and the wave crests were being blown back out to sea by a stiff easterly breeze. The aqua greens and blues changed on the waves, some with rooster tails, as his perspective changed from one curve to the next. Jared had never seen a painting or even a photo that could capture those wave and water colors. A few had come close but none had succeeded in doing justice to the beauty of the sun shining through breaking waves.

A whale spouted just outside the breaker line near Sea Lion Caves. He wondered how Tim was doing, stationed at Fort Bragg the last he'd heard. He also missed Bobby already and regretted not inviting him on the trip. He pulled off and watched, spotting three more of the behemoths traveling north. The east wind was cold, a refreshing though chilly change from the southwest rainy winds he had experienced for most of the winter. He found that he had the capacity to stay out on the overlook in comfort while other early spring tourists shuffled back to their cars quickly to snuggle their heaters and get warm again. He supposed that he was just used to being outside and was at home with the elements.

He stopped in Florence, on the Siuslaw River, and had a burger and fries at the DQ. He savored the old fashioned French fries that were so hard to find anymore. As an Indian kid he had grown up with food cooked in deep grease. He still loved it even though he knew it was bad for him. He sipped a Pepsi, glad to be freed at least for a time from the throes of alcohol. He wondered if the sugar in the pop was helping him to stay clear of the stuff.

He remembered the teachings of the drug and alcohol counselor who had told him about THIQ, the chemical that's found in heroin and also in alcohol. *Good Lord, how can they even sell that stuff?* He pondered these things as he herded his old Ford down the paved road toward the mighty Rogue.

He pushed south to an early stop at Tachenich Lake where he found a small camp spot on the back side of the lake away from pretty much everything. He rolled his air mattress and bag out in the back of the pickup, then picked up his fly rod and went fishing.

His first cast, using a floating hand-tied popper, was successful. A largemouth bass, of a pound or so, hit with astonishing power. The fight was short but sweet, with the bass pulling hard toward the safety of the lily pads it had emerged from. Jared landed the little fighter on the beach and kept him for dinner.

Two more bass, apparently in the same age group, took his fly within a dozen casts. He cleaned them and kept them as well.

Since he and Sherri had stayed up all night, he took a midday nap. Tired as he was, he couldn't get her face out of his mind. It was a beautiful face, and she possessed an inner beauty that had ambushed his heart. He knew he could get lost in her eyes if he let himself. *Who am I kidding?* he thought to himself. *I'm already lost—or maybe found ...* He drifted off to sleep.

When he woke from his nap he built a small

fire, broke out his frying pan, and went to work making dinner of bass fillets, fried potatoes with onions, canned pork and beans, and ice cold milk from his Coleman cooler. After supper he cleaned up, set a good-sized log on his fire, and sat in his folding chair enjoying the sunset as it disappeared into the western fog bank. He had made the right decision and would seek life and get away from death, at least for a while. He needed it deep in his soul; Jared hoped he still had one.

He again thought of Sherri as he tended his campfire that evening. She was something special, someone special. He remembered the Circle leader's instruction about tribal men "objectifying" tribal women, how we held our women "cheap" when we did that.

He was almost afraid to think of the possibilities with such a woman as Sherri. She could be the one: "the one." He couldn't help but compare her with Lisa. The difference was astounding to Jared. Where Sherri was quiet and gentle, Lisa was loud and ready to fight. Where Sherri was seeking Creator and His will for her life, Lisa was hard and in need of no one. Where Sherri listened to him and tried to understand, Lisa needed to be heard, understood, and taken care of. The difference was too great to measure. Jared knew that Sherri was special, very special. He had never known anyone like her before.

He didn't dare think about her anymore to-night. If he did he would be up all night; or maybe he would break camp and head back to Siletz, to her.

Sherri was pitching hay to Uncle John's cows, be-ing careful not to waste the quality grasshay. Two flakes per cow, "in the manger, not in the mud," he had instructed her. The cows ate with that steady plodding way that cows have. She had been here for six months now and knew how to feed cows and horses, gather eggs, wait on customers at the market, and teach Sunday school at the church. Life was better.

She thought of Jared as she worked, cleaning the horse stalls. He was different somehow, not out for himself like most of the guys are, trying to get into a girl's pants before they even know her name. His eyes told a different story, a story of possibili-ties. He seemed to be looking for a friend rather than a casual lover. It seemed to her that he was just waking up from a long sleep. He was gentle in his speech and careful with her. He made her feel valuable. That was so refreshing. She wondered, dared to wonder, if Jared was God's choice for her.

A logger? An alcoholic logger? An Indian? She had nothing against Indian people but understood that Jared had a bad reputation. Could he ever believe in God the way she did? She also knew that the Lord could perform miracles. Well, perhaps she should just pray for one, a really big one.

She knelt down in the freshly cleaned horse stall and did just that. "Heavenly Father, it's me, Sherri ..."

25

Water Flowing Deep

The next day, Jared Spotted-Horse stopped off at Port Orford—previously known as Fort Orford back in the old days of the Indian wars—and read the plaque at Battle Rock State Park. The history of the battle between his aboriginal ancestors and Captain Tichenor's sailors and settlers brought up some old anger. He saw in his mind's eye little glimpses of the fighting, the crew of the sea coaster *Seagull* popping up with rifles from the humps and brush of the rock, desperate, with their backs to the sea. He saw howling tribal warriors climbing the rock, shooting bows, hoping to rid the land of these invaders once and for all, ducking and dodging, as rifles and fowling pieces were discharged in their direction. He imagined the smoke, the war hoops, and the fire from the blazing muzzles. Then he saw and heard the five-pound cannon, loaded with rocks, nails, and pieces of scrap iron, cut loose and blow several tribal warriors back through the air and down onto the sand and into the rolling surf. In his mind's eye he bore witness to the blood and the carnage, heard the screams and wails of his ancestors and their adversaries alike. He shook his head as if to rid himself of the painful images.

Jared had friends who participated in the Run-To-The-Rogue, a 250-mile relay run from Siletz to Oak Flats on the Lower Illinois River, which joins with the Rogue about three miles downstream from the camp. Oak Flats was one of the main camps back in the 1800s, and for thousands of years before that. He had participated for the first time last year as part of his treatment plan. He had been allowed to carry the Eagle Staff. It was a powerful spiritual experience for him, the first he had ever had, and he hoped to take part again next year.

Jared wondered about something: At Port Orford the townspeople prepared a wonderful meal for the tribal runners. They provided different types of meats, potatoes, salads, pastas, breads, and assorted drinks free of charge. This was a feast! He was having a hard time figuring out what that was all about. Were these people trying to make peace, or to celebrate a peace they already had? It was his understanding that they had done this for years now. Both sides lost people in those battles, especially the last one here at Battle Rock. Jared was perplexed. Of course, none of the present-day people had been there; they were six or seven generations removed by now. So could it be just a novelty? Somehow he didn't think so. It just felt like something more serious than that. Perhaps the Creator was orchestrating something here? Could it be forgiveness? Were the good people of Port Orford feeding the good wolf and not the bad? He wondered.

The mouth of the Rogue River was beautiful, majestic when he crossed the bridge later that afternoon. Waves were breaking clear across the bar, pushing fluffy white foam into the bay with the incoming tide. It reminded Jared of yellow-white pillows floating in the blue-green water. Gulls circled above the turbulent tide rip with predatory eyes in search of herring, smelt, and oil-rich anchovies.

He chose to drive up the south road after gassing up and checking the oil and water. He stocked up on a few groceries since he knew prices upriver were restrictively high.

He imagined Sherri sitting beside him, smiling and holding his hand while he drove the pickup upriver on the bumpy narrow road. He felt silly but happy for the thought of her and hoped something could come of it. He shook his head, remembering his dark alcoholic history; he had his doubts about any kind of future with her. One day at a time didn't leave a lot of room for long-range planning or commitments. He knew he didn't have much to offer a woman, especially a God-fearing one. Clearly she was out of his league.

Several boats were plying the waters above the Rogue River Bridge for spring Chinook. He made a quick reconnaissance of those boats but saw no bent rods or waving nets. "Fishing must be slow," he announced to himself as the old Ford worked its way upriver.

The weather was warming. He rolled his window down and enjoyed the warmth and earthy, fresh smell of the big river while he listened to Willie Nelson croon: "Blue sky, shinin' on me ... nuthin' but blue sky—do I see ..."

He hadn't felt this lighthearted in quite a while. The Rogue always did that to him. It was like coming home after a long trip to a cold and foreign place. He wondered if it would always be like this for him. He wondered if old Chief John had felt the same way. He couldn't help considering the plight of the old tyees—the chiefs, trying to do the best they could in the face of a never-ending encroachment from the "Boston men" who were never satisfied. They pushed farther and farther into the homeland, raping and plundering as they went. How did the tyees, Sam and Limpy, Jack and Joe, deal with all the hard decisions in the hope of preventing the total extermination of their people? John, of course, Tecumtum, fought to the bitter end. He suffered for it too. So did his family. One of his sons was killed. Another lost a leg. Tyee John and his son Adam were cut down with swords and muskets, barely escaping with their lives. They had to endure four years of prison in Alcatraz on San Francisco Bay for defending their land and their families. They had been deemed "war criminals." Jared decided to camp at one of John's old camp sites and seek a healing.

Old Tyee John was Jared's personal hero. He loved the story of John and Adam and their attempt to forcefully take control of the steamer that was transporting them to Alcatraz. They almost got the job done but were finally overwhelmed by sheer numbers and superior firepower. Adam was cut down with a sword and John was shot with a musket. It had been a tough fight. Jared wondered how things might have turned out differently for his people had old John actually taken control of the ship and its crew.

He put his right arm across the seat back,

wishing she were there riding with him, helping him in his quest. He missed her already. "Stop it, Jared—she's too good for you. Just shake it off!"

He thought of Timmy, one of his very best friends in the world. Yes, he was white with flaming red hair, but he had the heart of a warrior. Tim was off doing who-knows-what with the Marine Corps. You just didn't get much more of a warrior's heart than that. If Tim had been around, Jared would've asked him to come and be with him at this special time. He had always been able to depend on Tim regardless of how tough things got. So, it was possible to get very close to a white man. *Yep, we're more like brothers than friends.* He missed him.

The paved river road was cracked and in bad disrepair for mile after mile. He took this as a sign that not too many people used it these days. Very little logging took place in the Rogue country anymore since the clear-cut ban on federal timberlands. That was fine with Jared. He had always felt that the cutting had been too fast and furious anyway. Despite his logger status, he liked trees, the bigger the better, especially the giant old-growth fir and Sitka spruce.

He thought of his grandpa and uncles on his mother's side who had felled the giant trees with razor-sharp crosscut saws. They notched the stumps and hung springboards, climbing as high as fifteen to eighteen feet and balancing on those narrow boards while they plied the tools of their trade, the double-bitted falling axes, the crosscut saws, the hammer and steel wedges, even that little jar of kerosene that eased the saw bind in the cut. He still had an old crosscut saw that an uncle had given him. He had even kept the little Coke bottle that held the kerosene.

Jared could almost smell the turpentine-like aroma of the pitch and the sweet scent of raw-wood sawdust. He could almost hear the saw teeth dragging the flaked yellow wood out of the cuts. He imagined it cascading out both sides of the cut and floating with the breeze. The crackling of the breaking hinge wood and then the age-old faller's call—"Timber!"—were loud in his mind. The call was followed by the earth-shaking crash of the monster tree violently impacting the ground, then driving itself into a furrowed bed and settling down to await the bucker's saw that would cut it into log lengths. He imagined it being yarded to the donkey, loaded onto railroad cars, and taken to town via steam-driven train engine.

Man, those were the days! Jared thought. Giant old-growth timber, in stands so thick that the light couldn't penetrate to the ground, centuries old, had endured storms of wind, snow, ice, and rain. He had heard the stories from the old ones, including Uncle Ree, about the pure majesty of the spruce stands that had graced the near-coast lands. Only pictures could come close to doing justice to them. Words were just too weak. His mind came back to the present.

His old Ford carried him across the Illinois River; he glanced upstream toward Oak Flats, the old tribal encampment. He felt a little tug at his heart as he saw the house built on what he knew had been a tribal burial ground at one time. "Chi-islu, daydaat'e." He hadn't used the old words for "place-of-the-dead" in years. Well, he was back on the Rogue—Tolhut Talihee—what could he expect? And who was *really* dead, the bodies in the burial ground or the "hiine" who built the house on the sacred place? Jared found himself starting to think in spiritual terms, a throwback from his bloodline and the early teaching of Uncle Ree.

He looked left, across the river, and saw the Agness airstrip, slanted downward like the back of a dog's neck. He was amazed at the short strip built into the hillside. It looked more than a little dangerous. But since he didn't plan on flying in or out of there, it made no difference to him. He hoped to see a plane land or take off there one of these days, just to see how it was done.

Jared stopped the pickup in a wide spot and

stepped to the edge of the road, overlooking the river. He watched a white and speckled osprey fly upriver, hunting for fish. He glanced way up high in the sky and spotted a lone bald eagle circling in afternoon thermal. He envied the bird its view of the river and the valley. It did a little wing dip and quickly switched direction, then resumed its smooth, circling thermal climb. "Show off," he grinned.

He was thinking about camping up at Bear Camp, one of his favorite campsites, but decided not to. *There is just too much chance of snow in the high country this time of year*, he thought. He opted to make camp on Shasta Costa Creek in a little meadow that was well hidden and had been one of old Tecumtum's favorite encampments. He did just that, creeping in slowly so as to avoid hitting the boulders hidden in the tall orchard grass. He followed an old Jeep trail and maneuvered to within fifty feet of the old tribal camp, abandoned only after the last battle drove the people from the valley a century and a half before. It was the perfect camp, nestled in a grove of ancient oak trees and surrounded by the gurgling Shasta Costa Creek. Jared set to work and made a good solid camp. He planned to be there a few days.

Dusk was descending when he settled in and built his evening fire, admiring the fine camp replete with tent, fire pit, table, chair, and, of course, the inevitable clothesline. He quieted himself as the fire began crackling and licking away at the kindling wood, contrasting against full darkness. He added a couple of bigger chunks of madrone, placed just right, so that when the kindling burned down the larger split wood would fall into the coals, making for a hotter, more durable flame with the added benefit of beautiful rainbow colors.

A coyote howled in the west as the sun settled over the ridge, dropping down through the Douglas and Noble firs toward the Pacific Ocean, to sizzle away into nothingness.

He remembered the "coyote" stories Uncle Ree used to tell on the hunting trips around the campfire at night. Coyote was always fooling Bear and Cougar, using his wits to stay one step ahead of the larger and stronger animals. Coyote always ended up with a full belly while Bear and Cougar went hungry. It seemed like Coyote took a lot of chances just to get out of a little work. He knew people like that too; he wondered if he was one of them.

Deep down, Jared suspected that he had some coyote in him. He had drunk too much for too long and had "coyoted" some of his own people. He wasn't proud of what he had done. He had stolen money, jewelry, even guns from his family in

order to feed his addictions. He had lied, manipu-
lated, cheated, and betrayed. He knew he couldn't
fix any of it. He was helpless to undo the damage.
Better not to think of it so much. He could hear the
words of Uncle Ree: *Time to sleep.* He wondered if
Sherri thought of him as a coyote. He hoped not.
He really hoped not.

Jared woke up trembling in the dark. Daylight
was just breaking when he unzipped the sleeping bag and rolled to his knees, not bothering to
dress, shivering from the morning cold—*or was it
the dream?*

He had dreamed of the old ones, fighting on the
ridge above Big Bend of the River. They had held
off the soldiers for a time. Tecumtum and his warriors were eventually outflanked and overwhelmed.
That was the last battle his people fought. The end
of freedom came after that. Since then, the tribes
had been enslaved to whatever demon had come
along, with alcohol at the head of the charge and,
nowadays, meth a close second.

He waded into freezing Shasta Costa Creek
and sat on a large round rock that he somehow
knew had been used for this purpose countless
times before. He bathed himself, wondering if
this was a sign of things to come. He knew in his
heart just how sick and dirty he really was. He was
sicker and dirtier inside than out. He poured the

shockingly cold water over his head, allowing it to cascade down his back. He felt the goose bumps rise as he hand-cupped more onto his chest and stomach, his legs and knees. He sat there silently, listening to the songbirds of the morning. A crow called in the distance as if to say "Dirty, dirty, still dirty."

Jared hoped it was wrong and that it was just a black-colored bird making meaningless noises. But he knew better.

The warming fire was wonderful. He turned himself around like a squirrel roasting on a spit. He had always loved the crackling of the fire and the smoke that "always followed beauty."

Jared found some cedar boughs and made a smudge like the old ones had done for purification. He never had believed in the old ways but was somehow comforted by it in his morning ablution. The smell of the burning cedar was acrid sweet and powerful to his nostrils, causing his head to lighten and his eyes to burn.

He turned away for fresh air and caught a fleeting glimpse of a very large cinnamon-colored bear. He watched as it lumbered slowly and powerfully across the edge of his camp clearing and disappeared into the conifers, almost as though it were a part of the smoke and had never been there at all.

He sat by his fire as the morning light turned to sunshine, sipping his coffee and breathing deep of the natural aromas of the Rogue River Valley, the riparian abundance of the Shasta Costa, and the warming-up smells of the morning. "Shum!" So good.

26

Fishing the Rogue

After a breakfast of Raisin Bran and black coffee, Jared unlimbered his old fly rod and headed for the river. His camp was only a half mile up Shasta Costa Creek from the Rogue. He hiked the trail along the creek and fished the Rogue at the confluence. Selecting a #12 Royal Wolfe, he false cast a half dozen times, stripping line on each back cast, and laid the little colorful dry fly at the edge of the rippled water of the creek where it met with the slower, darker water of the river.

Trout were slurping mayflies off the surface, boiling the water into a sunlit froth. Jared salivated as he made his cast, presenting the little coachman pattern with precision. He was rewarded with the smashing strike of a spring "half-pounder," a rainbow trout of about sixteen inches. The fight lasted several minutes with the red-sided trout using every trick in the book, sliding into heavy current, turning sideways, and sounding into the deep but finally succumbing to the unrelenting tension of the Fenwick rod and the Shasta Costa man caressing it.

He fished for the better part of the morning, catching, releasing, fighting fish in the most sporting and exciting way he knew—with a fly rod, ultralight leader, and barbless hooks. He had tied the flies himself as part of his personal therapy toward sobriety. They were all like him, individually different and each flawed in its own way. But they caught fish.

He kept one for the pan and felt no guilt about it since it was all part of the circle of life, or so he had been taught when very young. By whom? Uncle Ree? Some other elder? Perhaps his grandfather, who had died when Jared was just a few years old? He really didn't remember; but no matter. He knew this to be true.

He spent his afternoons gathering wood, wandering the trails above the creek, and learning the lay of the land. His evenings were quiet times of reflection and solitude.

He had no right to think of Sherri in the way he did, imagining a future together, a family; but he did anyway. He saw her eyes in the waters of the river. He saw her smile in the rising sun. He saw her everywhere.

But she was a white girl. He knew lots of mixed marriages; most of them had failed. He also knew himself and how he could let people down—he remembered all the people he *had* let down. But her eyes were two aqua blue-green pools of hope and whispered dreams. He heard her gentle laughter in the gurgling riffles. He dared to think of love. So he considered the possibility of marrying her, having kids, loving her. After all, Timmy was white, as white as they got, and his heart was good. Jared pondered the future.

His nights were spent in battle, fighting from the foxholes, yelling and screaming and shooting. He often heard the screams of the dying and witnessed the spilling of their blood. The horrible sounds would continue even after he woke in the morning, and he would lie trembling in his sleeping bag until the last scream drifted off with the darkness of the night. The nightmare always ended the same way: the people were taken to pens of thick steel wire where they drank alcohol and fought each other. He was always in the dream, drinking alcohol and laughing a coyote laugh. His mother was in the dream. She always looked at him with tears in her eyes, shaking her head from side to side. Bobby was there too, saying, "My people die for lack of vision."

Lying there in the dawn, he knew: yes, without a doubt he knew that he was slowly but steadily moving toward insanity. Someday the dream would not stop with the daylight; he would be trapped in battle on the smoke-fogged ridgetop and would spend eternity in the blood-drenched foxhole. He would be drunk and unable to sober up or stand and fight for his people. He would remain … Coyote. "Sk'um."

27

How Does One Seek Vision?

He wasn't here to fish for trout or scout out old trails or relax in the springtime sun. He was here for his Spirit Quest; in his counseling he had reached the step where he must recognize a "power greater than himself." Dare he say Creator? He knew in his heart that this was key to addressing those tormenting nightmares that were now spilling over into the light of day and threatening to consume his soul. The trouble was, he didn't believe. He had tried, but he just couldn't truly believe in God or Creator—or much of anything or anyone for that matter. He had been let down by so many, so often, for so long. He felt that we were all just here for a time and then gone. End of story.

How could one pray to a God or a Creator who

either did not exist or was distant and uncaring, allowing terrible things to happen to the people?

How to begin a process of praying and purifying? How would a heathen prepare? He, Jared Spotted-Horse, had never been one to pray. What he knew about praying had to do with Christian people, the same ones who had taken the land using their Bible and their Manifest Destiny (God's plan to save the heathens by spreading the Gospel) to rob his people of all things good. He thought that perhaps there was nothing left of his people.

The statistics he had learned in Circle angered him. How could someone claim to love God or Creator or Jesus and at the same time rob, steal, rape, murder, and destroy a whole race of people? It made no sense! And how could he pray to a Creator who would allow such a terrible thing? It was confusing and enraging at the same time. Yet, he knew in his heart that he must try. Jared was out of options. His sanity was leaving him. He had no joy, no hope. Even his thoughts of Sherri were futile. He knew he would blow it somehow, get drunk, get thrown in jail, hurt her somehow. He knew it as surely as he knew his father had deserted him and his mother had drunk herself into an early grave.

Or he might do to her what Bob Sr. had done to Missy. She was a beautiful lady until Bob got done with her. Now she hobbled around, missing several teeth, her hair graying. Her left eye drooped. Her left leg drug behind her in a pitiful fashion. "Oh God, could I ever do that to Sherri?"

He remembered the old ones telling the stories, the horrible, almost unthinkable stories of Ben Wright, the great "Indian Killer," who went about poisoning the Tututnis, Shasta Costas, Klamaths, Modocs, and many others with his free haunches of beef: poisoned beef laced with strychnine. Poison. The great Indian Killer was nothing more than a sneak and a thief who took what he wanted after killing the warriors with his poison.

But Old Chief John had seen through this man's deception. He had recognized the evil heart in Ben Wright. John and his warriors had ridden into his camp while the haunches of beef were roasting and giving off their rich aroma, beckoning all to come and feast and make peace-talk. Many warriors had accepted Wright's offer of free beef and good palaver. But John and his small band of rugged warriors had ridden off, spitting on Ben Wright's forked-tongued offer of peace and goodwill.

Those warriors who stayed and ate the poisoned meat were shot and stabbed while writhing on the ground in agony. Their women were raped and then killed. Their children and elders were slaughtered. The great Indian Killer had struck again.

"But how had Tyee John known? Was it spirit? Was it vision?"

Jared had to make the nightmares stop. If praying belonged to the old way—perhaps Chief John's way, part of the ancient process—then so be it. He could feel himself slipping into something akin to a deep depression, an abyss that had no bottom. He saw Sherri's face. He was comforted by it. But even her face couldn't stop his inevitable slide toward insanity. He was slipping away. He knew it but couldn't stop it.

28

Smudging at Shasta Costa Creek

His little fire was adequate to burn the cedar boughs. He had smudged with sweet grass and eagle feathers in Circle and other tribal functions but he didn't have those things now. He had a campfire and cedar boughs and that is what he used.

He uttered a prayer as he stood in the cedar smoke, turning around so it would cover all parts of his body. He and his hunting partners had smoked themselves in this same way in order to cover their man-smell before a hunt. It really did help a hunter get close to animals if the wind was swirling and unpredictable. But he had never done anything like this for purely spiritual reasons. He hoped it would protect him from evil spirits, hiding him while he was weak from fasting, praying,

and going without sleep. He hoped the purification would take and he would be found worthy of
a vision.

He stood with the smoke encapsulating him.
He turned and prayed, asking to be purified and
made ready to receive a vision. He opened his eyes
and caught a glimpse of a cinnamon-colored bear
stealthily moving, skirting the edge of his camp.
It was there for a moment, then obscured by the
smoke, then gone, slipping into the timber and
away. *Was it the same bear?* he wondered.

"Creator, purify me in the old way. Clean my
mind and heart so when I come for a vision there
will be one for me. I am sick. I am 'sk'um.' Help
me."

Uncle Ree had told him to do that every morning and every night for six days, and on the sev-
enth go and seek a high place to fast and pray until
he was given a vision, even if it took several days.
He didn't know how to do it. He had never received any formal instruction; but perhaps, hopefully, he knew enough to try. Whatever it took to
get a good night's sleep again, he would do. And so
he did, every day, smoking and purifying himself.

"Creator, help me. Sherri, pray for me … Uncle Ree, I wish you were here … Timmy, Bobby …
Mom … Jack?"

He had heard the old ones talk about Vision

Quest; he knew that an uncle, a father, or a grand-father usually accompanied a young man at his coming of age, around twelve or thirteen, sometimes fourteen, depending on when he reached puberty. But Jared had no one to accompany him, to keep watch over him from a distance. He wondered if that old rite of passage was gone for good.

Terry Red Bear told of his father, who had gone on Vision Quest years ago. His father's uncle had followed him, kept track of him from another ridge, and had made a secret camp. The uncle had crept close to keep watch as the young man spread his blanket, fasted, prayed, smudged, and cried out to Creator for a true vision. It had taken four days, but a vision had come. A new name had come as a result of the vision. Afterward the uncle had cared for him, given him water, and probably saved his life.

That vision seeker had lived to be an old man. He had given much of himself to the people, serving on tribal council, going to Washington, D.C., to speak to Congress, and raising a family on the reservation. His vision had been real and good. This gave Jared much hope as he prepared for his quest. He wondered if any on the Siletz Tribal Council had sought vision. He suspected at least some had.

Jared had given serious thought to asking Uncle Ree to come watch over him while he fasted and prayed, but he knew in his heart that his favorite uncle was just too old to take on such a chore. He loved him too much to ask.

He knew he needed someone to trail him, possibly to care for him, on his trip up the mountain. He decided to pray for someone to watch over him on his endeavor to find vision. If given a vision he didn't want to die or wander off over a cliff or simply become lost in the rugged entrapments of the Rogue River country.

29

The Helper

On the afternoon of the sixth day, a man came into his camp with a pack on his back. He was older than Jared by ten years or so, clearly a man of the outdoors, rugged in looks and dress.

He wore a crusher felt hat, a lambskin vest over a work shirt, denim jeans and lace-up boots, a pair of old work gloves in his back pocket. His hair was medium-long for he was clearly of Indian descent. His complexion held the ruddiness of a mixed breed with the weathered look of one who spent his time outdoors. But Jared could only make a guess based on the mixed breeds he knew back on the rez, including himself.

Jared saw him coming through the meadow on the east side of camp, navigating the trail easily, carefully, taking his time and watching the ground as though he gathered as he traveled. He stopped, reached down and picked up something, an acorn perhaps, and dropped it into a small pouch hanging from his belt, then moved on into the camp, calling out a greeting as he entered Jared's little clearing next to the creek.

"Hello the camp. May I come in?" asked the stranger.

"Come on in," invited Jared. "Come in and have coffee with me. I have some fish, too, if you're hungry and don't mind my cooking," he said as he moved to the pickup to get another folding chair out of the back.

He took note of this guy, clearly some sort of bush Indian, as he set up his chair and moved to get him a cup of camp coffee from the pot balanced on the flat fire-pit rock. He poured the black liquid into a blue enamel tin cup and presented it to the clearly grateful guest.

"I been on the trail for a good while. Came down through the Illinois trail then swung up to the Indigo Canyon country. Just worked my way down Shasta Costa Creek drainage. You're the first guy I seen in near two weeks. Glad to have the coffee and the company." He sipped the coffee, savoring the smell and the warmth of the tin cup in his weathered hands.

Jared studied him as he sipped the coffee. He sensed something special about this fellow, as though a kinship existed even before an exchange of names took place.

"I'm Jared Spotted-Horse, up from the Siletz country, taking some time off. Glad to meet you."

"Same here, Jared. People call me Shad. Among other things I'm a mix of different tribes. My mom was Jewish. My dad was, well, the stories vary. Let's leave it at that. I'm a long ways from home. Been on the trail a while now."

Jared wondered if this fellow was wanted by the law. He hadn't given his full name. He had a hard look in his physical features, not really very big, maybe 160 pounds or so. He had kind eyes though, knowing eyes with laugh wrinkles around the edges. Clearly Shad liked to laugh. He also had a rough and ruddy complexion, a formidable nose, and sharp eyes. And he could use a good washing.

He apparently did wash though, since he had no rank odor about him. A man had to take care of himself, even when out in the tall and uncut for long periods of time, so he didn't get sick or tick-bit. Cleanliness was essential to living out and about.

"I see ya been smokin' cedar. Mind if I ask what that's all about?"

Jared thought some before replying to the overly direct question. He didn't know this guy from Adam and already he had asked a question that was, well, personal. But what was the harm in answering? He was just passing through. He appeared to be a free spirit, perhaps a wanderer, maybe a guy on the run from the realities and harshness of modern day life.

"Preparing for Vision Quest." He peered into Shad's eyes for a moment, then looked down, as though ashamed he hadn't done this years ago. He doubted Shad even knew what Vision Quest meant.

"My cousin John helped me when I did my Vision Quest. I was twelve, just a kid. I never shared with anybody what I seen, but I seen plenty. Powerful stuff—powerful vision. I went up into some high country and spent many days seeking Creator's vision for my life. It was hard, cold, long; and it was real good. You're going down a good trail there, Jared. I hope you find that vision. The people perish for lack of vision, ya know."

He was astonished at Shad's words. Had he read his thoughts somehow? *Did he have an auntie who said those kinds of things to him?* he wondered.

They talked late into the night, becoming friends. Fish were fried and eaten; stories were shared. Shad talked of his upbringing in a logging and carpentry family. He told of his time using an axe, hand saw, and splitting maul. Jared was amazed that Shad could speak the old Chinook Jargon trade language. He shared that he could speak many languages and had done so for years. "A gift," he said, "and a curse." He winked.

Jared could relate, not to Shad's gift of languages but to his stories. They were different men and yet the same. Jared had seen a book called *Stranger in a Strange Land*. He had always wondered what the book was about. He had never read it but suspected that it was something he would relate to if he ever did.

The fire was just embers when Shad rolled out his bedroll and climbed in. Jared turned into his own in the back of the pickup. It had been a good evening; Jared had an idea, but would sleep on it.

Jared awoke with a start: the dream again. He shook himself, drew in a sharp breath of cold morning air, and rolled out of his bag, slipping his shoes on. As his shod feet hit the ground he smelled smoke and coffee, the aroma drawing him to the crackling fire. He noted Shad, bent over the cooking fire, deftly flipping a trout with a flat stick as though he'd had years of practice. Jared had seen short-order cooks make little moves like that. The only cooks he knew personally had picked up the culinary arts in prison classes. He wondered.

"Come and get it, sleepyhead. I caught some trout, made up some fry bread too. I hope you don't mind me using your rod. By the way, it's a nice one. Did you tie those flies?"

Jared nodded, feeling a little funny that a stranger would use his gear without asking first. But he let it pass in light of the fact that Shad would have had to wake him in order to ask.

Jared took the cup from Shad's extended hand. The steam carried a rich aroma. Folgers had never tasted so good.

"What did you do to this coffee?" asked Jared.

"Thought you might like it. I pick kanikanick along the trail, dry it, then crumble it up for a coffee drink. Sometimes I just add it to whatever coffee is available. It really adds something, don't ya think?"

"It sure does. I'll have to get you to show me how. This is really good, better than Starbuck's."

"Glad you like it, Jare."

Jared was surprised that Shad used the nickname his friends back home used. He guessed it wasn't all that unusual a nickname, given his name and the natural way to shortening it. It seemed as though he had known Shad for years, like an old friend, a kindred spirit. He was surprised at himself. He generally wasn't this trusting. He had been when he was a little kid, but that wore off quickly enough.

They ate their fish and bread with gusto, enjoying the coffee while the cool morning thermal carried the aromas of the high country down into their camp and onto the great river below.

"You been gettin' ready for this awhile. Wanna go up and find your sacred place today? Get started with that Vision Quest?"

Shad asked the question very matter-of-factly, as though it was a normal thing to discuss. He could just as easily have asked if Jared wanted a refill on the coffee.

"Today is the day. I'm ready. I just hope it's a real thing. It's like I'm drawn toward something but I'm afraid of what I might find, ya know?"

"I do. Had some similar thoughts myself many years ago. Let's get started. I'll take care of things here and come check on you every day, just to make sure you're doing OK. You won't even see me. I'll just get close, watch a while, then slip away when I'm sure all is well. That's the way they did it for me and it worked out fine. OK?"

"OK." Jared could hardly believe how this was going down. Should he trust this guy? Could he even trust his own judgment anymore? But he had prayed for help and Shad had shown up. Perhaps he was the answer to prayer after all.

30

The Sacred Place

They left camp on foot and headed downstream. They turned upstream when they got to the Rogue River. They hiked along the road that paralleled the stream, crossed a bridge, and headed upstream on the north side of the river. Shad led the way to an old trail that headed up onto a ridge of scrub oak and conifer timber. They climbed steadily for half an hour, topping out on a sharp ridge.

"What is this place?" asked Jared. It looked strangely familiar to him, as though he had been here many times before. The fact was he never had, at least not in this world. But sometimes the spirit world and the dream world come together in the quiet places of a man's mind.

"There was a battle here once, long ago. Your

people fought the soldiers. It was quite a battle, lasting for several days. It was the last major battle your people ever fought. Shortly after that they went to the reservation. Maybe you've heard of the Battle of the Big Bend?" Shad cocked his head as he asked, expecting a reaction from Jared.

"Yeah, I've heard of it. I never knew where it was. I just knew they fought and a lot of folks died on both sides. I never did really know the whole story though. This is where that happened?"

"Right on this spot. See the holes in the ground? Those are rifle pits. The soldiers dug them, kinda like a modern-day foxhole. See that knob over there? Your great grampas and great uncles and cousins were dug in there. That ridge to the left is where John, Adam, and his fighters were at. Your guys had the soldiers in a wicked crossfire for quite a while and nearly cut 'em to pieces. Yep, heckuva battle."

Jared felt a cold sense of recognition then. This was the place of his recurring dream. The trees were right; the ground was the way he remembered it. Even the smell of the place was familiar, as though he knew the aromas, the grasses, the pines, every fragrance of this place. What did it mean? He didn't know.

"Jared, let's say a prayer here. This is a sacred

place if there ever was one. Go ahead and put your blanket out. This is a good place. Let's just take care of business right here."

Shad took a couple of things out of his pack and placed them on the blanket. He laid out an eagle feather, an abalone shell, two small bundles of dried sage, some matches, and an old wooden canteen filled with fresh water.

As he proceeded to put a sage bundle into the abalone shell, they both squatted on the blanket. Shad lit the sage and winnowed air onto it with the eagle feather. As the smoke began to rise he directed it with the feather into the ceremonial "smudge" of purification. He feathered the smoke onto his heart and head and prayed quietly to himself. He handed the shell to Jared, who proceeded to purify himself in the old way.

Shad spoke. "Creator, we ask for a good vision for my brother Jared. We ask that he be taken to the spirit place that You have for him. We ask that his vision be powerful and good. We ask that he bring this vision to the people when it is time. We know that all visions are given so the people may be served and may be saved. Thank you Grandfather, Chief Cornerstone. Aho."

With that Shad got up and left the ridge top, leaving Jared to seek his vision and new name and thereby become a whole person, a true warrior, a servant of his people, and a man of spirit, strong in the ways of Creator.

Jared wondered, "How can a nonspiritual non-believer receive anything of value here? And who is Chief Cornerstone?" He concluded that desperation had driven him to this. Here and now was his last hope. He knew he would die for lack of vision. He considered the possibility that he had already gone insane and that this was all a part of his insanity.

31

Seeking Vision

He began by praying quietly on the old wool blanket, asking for a true vision. He moved from his knees to a squatting position to a prone position, on his face. He used the water in the canteen for drinking, which he did sparingly. His prayers were very stumbling. He struggled on with it.

He lay on his back and looked up through the leaves and needled branches of the trees. He noted the slight breeze blowing through the tops, causing them to sway like a dancer, dreaming and moving slowly to the beat of the unheard music. He felt like Uncle Ree, lying down and looking up through the Tall and Uncut.

He regretted eating the trout for breakfast but then thought better of it. It was a good fish and quite tasty. The fast was for purification. That trout had not been impure, to his way of thinking. Besides, was the Creator so fickle as to care about such a thing as eating a trout?

The first day passed quietly. He never spoke verbally but only in his mind. His prayers became gentle and childlike. "Grandfather, I just want to do what's right. I don't want to do bad things anymore. Help me by showing me. You are the Power. You are the Hammer. You are the Knowing One. I am not." He came to realize that he was being taught how to pray by someone or something greater than himself. The day passed quickly, with the evening light losing its way in the darkness that rose up quietly in stealth. He thought he caught a quick glimpse of Shad but couldn't be sure.

The stars came out and shone down through the treetops. The contrast of cobalt blue sky and silver-studded stars was almost overwhelming to Jared's tired eyes. He felt his body weakening. Yet he didn't feel weak in his mind or his heart. On the contrary, he began to feel a strength, an inner strength, that he had never felt before. He could not explain it to himself; but it was so. *Is this the good wolf overcoming the evil wolf?* he wondered as the stars twinkled and spoke volumes to his soul.

He prayed quietly, now verbally, as the sun rose. He began moving into a quiet place where he no longer heard the chirping of birds, where the sounds of the wind faded away, where the river sounds were gone. He prayed and slipped into a better place without realizing it, crossing back and forth into two worlds, both real but dimensionally separate.

He heard Bobby's cackling laugh. He saw Uncle Ree telling a story of a big buck that had outsmarted them all. He saw Tony around a fire, telling a hunting story, dancing and jumping as though he were a giant buck running through the broken ground of heavy timber. He saw Timmy swinging a baseball bat and grinning. He saw his mother's eyes just before she died, pleading for understanding. She was shaking her head from side to side and moving her mouth, making inaudible sounds.

Jared came awake on the blanket, looked around, saw that it was dusk. He heard the scampering sound of a small animal in the brush. The sun was just dipping into the west and the shadows were growing larger, taller—whether for the third or fourth time, he didn't know or care. He pulled the blanket around his shoulders, took a small sip of the water, and closed his eyes, feeling himself slipping away slowly into that other world, the quiet world, the world of the inner mind, the soul. He felt a peace envelope him softly, like a warm feather pillow. Time lost all meaning. It no longer existed for him. He was crossing over into that which only the few can cross and return from. He had no idea that the sun was setting on the third day. He drifted off.

Jack smiled at him. He was wearing his hard hat, standing on a sunlit hillside, waving. A breeze was blowing, causing his hair to move like the ripples in a golden shimmering pond. His smile was as big and warm as ever. His eyes shone with joy. He stood straight and tall, strong in the morning sun. He laughed and the sound of it echoed off the surrounding slopes. He was happy and whole. His wounds were gone. Jack was alive and well. He fairly beamed.

Jared rose from the blanket and stood facing Jack. He tried to speak but was unable. How could this be? It was clearly Jack, Preacher Jack. How had he gotten here on the Rogue? To Tolhut Tahilee?

The giant Bear moved toward Jared, coming slowly, deliberately, its big head swinging from side to side as though heavy and powerful. Beside the Bear was a Man wearing the old tribal regalia. His hair was black and adorned with beautifully plumed eagle feathers. His chest was covered with seashells and strings of dentilium. Jared recognized the dentilium as the tube-shaped seashells that were a designation of great riches. He also wore strings of wampum, ancient money. His feet were shod in beaded moccasins, beautiful in their craftsmanship and simple in a rose design. He walked with an air of majesty and power, unafraid.

Above the Man and the Bear flew an Eagle, magnificent in its ability to soar, circling and swooping, using the power of majestic wings. This was the great golden eagle, the most regal of all.

Flying around the Bear, the Man, and the Eagle were hundreds and thousands of birds, of all sizes, singing their songs, calling out, clearly in awe of the Three. They worshipped with all they had.

As the Bear, the Man, and the Eagle approached Jared he saw animals of all kinds looking in from the forest. They were surrounded by deer, elk, cougar, bobcat, bear, rabbits, squirrels, and even coyotes. Small rodents observed from the distance. The sky was blackened with all kinds of insects. The ground itself began to vibrate. They all moved in closer, drawn to the majestic Three.

He recognized some of the animals he had killed over the years. He saw the bear whose life he had taken in the orchard. It was healthy and very much alive, robust and unthreatening. It looked at him with the same recognition he had seen earlier. So he hadn't imagined it! He saw the cinnamon-colored bear that had moved through the outer edge of his smoke vision back in John's camp. Jared took note of a bull elk he had taken years before. It, too, was robust and watched the Trio that was approaching. He sensed no animosity toward him from the majestic elk. The bull tilted its antlers forward as though to bow. The other animals assumed postures of worship as well.

As the Three approached Jared, he couldn't help but feel the power of their presence. He wondered if he was awake or dreaming. He didn't feel fear, only wonder. Was this a vision? Was this a dream? Perhaps a hallucination?

The Man was clearly some kind of Chief but also a Warrior carrying weapons. His bow was simple as were His arrows. The quiver was of otter. The bow looked like yew wood with its deep red and contrasting soft white colors. It was what bowyers would recognize as a "flat bow," designed for short work from heavy cover or off the back of a running horse. Jared recognized the hunting flat bow of his own Shasta Costa Tribe.

The Warrior wore a knife with a white obsidian blade and an elk-antler grip. It was sheathed in a fringed elk hide adorned with beads, quills, and small gray seashells. He wore a breastplate of hair pipe bone and carried a golden pipe hawk in His red sash. He was, in a word, magnificent. In spite of all the scars on His body, He was beautiful, powerful, and, not surprisingly, gentle in speech.

The Great Bear dwarfed the Man, Whose head barely reached the shoulder of the Bear, which carried Himself on all fours. This was like no bear Jared had ever seen. His hair was a foot long, shining bright in shades of black and brown, blonde and red. His head was the size of a truck tire, His claws as long as a man's foot. This being was more than a bear. He exuded power in all directions and glowed with it as though electrically charged.

This magnificent animal did not communicate in any way Jared was familiar with, certainly not with a spoken language. But there was communication that bypassed his consciousness and penetrated directly with and deeply into his soul. He felt a great peace when he looked at the Great Bear. Jared felt safe.

The Eagle was at least three times as large as any eagle Jared had ever seen, with a wing span of twelve feet or more. The eyes were aglow as though charged with the same electricity as the giant Bear. Its movements were powerful, swift, and graceful, as though it was born by an unseen but extremely powerful force beyond any earthly wind.

Jared was overcome with the magnificence of what was before him and dropped to his face, quivering, in fear and in reverence. He was in the presence of something, Someone he had never even imagined, and was overwhelmed in every sense and every part of his being. He knew that he was in the presence of the Creator, a Creator he never could have envisioned, a being beyond description. A Creator he had never believed in.

The Man spoke.

"Jared, son of brokenness, stand up and greet your Creator."

Jared was stunned, unable to move, unable to breathe. He could only bow down and tremble at what he was experiencing. Somehow he was still able to reason within himself. He was doubting his own sanity now. Here before him stood a magnificent warrior decked out in full tribal regalia replete with beaded moccasins, quilled leggings, buckskin breech clout, bone pipe breastplate, buckskin-beaded gauntlets, absolutely stunning eagle feathers, and the most piercing eyes of any human being he had ever seen. Yes, he was in awe. He stood as commanded, barely able to keep his legs under him. What magnificence. What power! What majesty!

The Bear was more magnificent yet. It stood so tall, even on all fours, that the Man was dwarfed by It, yet He was very comfortable with It. The claws were curved downward and were, well, scary. Jared now came to understand that men must fear God. If this Bear was God, he was truly afraid. Yet he didn't feel that kind of fear but a deep and abiding respect and awe. He had no doubt that he could be destroyed instantly at the will of any of these Beings who were before him, but his fear was in his own lack, his own darkness and weakness, his own "coyoteness." He was beginning to see, to sense, the evil within himself. He realized he was trembling.

The Eagle swooped close, engulfing him in a swirling wind the likes of which he had never experienced before, and spoke gently to Jared, "Do not be afraid, for you are in the presence of the Creator. I AM the Messenger to those who love and serve Him. Do not be afraid, Jared. Have no fear. We have come to meet you between the worlds. You are in a good place, Jared Spotted-Horse."

He felt a peace go through him that had had no place in him before. He looked up into the eyes of the Bear, then the Eagle, and then into the eyes of the Man, who spoke to him.

"Jared, you have come seeking that which is greater than yourself. I have written to men in the Book of Heaven that 'If you seek Me you will find Me; if you knock, the door will be opened to you.' Do you understand who I AM?"

"You must be God, the Creator. But why are You a man, a bear, and an eagle? I don't understand this." Jared was amazed that he could speak at all. His trembling had ceased. The Man replied in a resounding and yet a gentle voice:

"I AM the only Son of Creator and a part of Him. If He were to show Himself to you in His true form, in His fullness, what men refer to as Holiness, you would be consumed, vaporized, in an instant. So He has chosen to appear in the form of the Great Bear. It was He who spoke into your heart and soul a few moments ago. This goes beyond language—it can only be understood and lived out in spirit for it is perfect truth.

"The Eagle is the messenger, and also a part of I AM, the One who is sent to comfort and to guide, to strengthen and empower, to enlighten, to interpret for and to inspire those who love and serve Creator, the Great I AM."

"And what of you?" Jared asked. "You come as a man, a traditional man of the tribes. Your regalia is excellent. You appear to be a warrior, perhaps a great chief of the people. I understand the Great Bear as GrandFather or Father Creator. I understand the Eagle as the One-Who-Brings-Prayers. But I don't understand you, a man of the tribes, who walks with Creator in your own right."

"I have revealed Myself to the people many

times in many ways throughout the generations and seasons of time. I AM a warrior, yes.
I AM also a teacher and One-who-tells-of the-
future. I AM also a healer. But most importantly, I
CAME to serve and to give Myself for the darkness
within the people. I CAME for the sick and the
brokenhearted. I CAME for you, Jared Spotted-
Horse, for you are in need of healing. I CAME to
save you from yourself. I AM the Sacrificial Warrior. All who follow the Creator are to live a life of
sacrifice, serving I AM by serving My people. The
Warrior always serves himself last, Jared. You are
called to this if you choose to follow Me. If you do
choose to follow me, I will require that you 'drive
your stake into the ground' and give yourself totally."

Jared understood the term "drive your stake
into the ground." Its meaning came from the old-
time Cheyenne Dog Soldiers who were the best
of the best in tribal warfare. Their charge was to
protect the people at all costs, including driving
a wooden stake or "sacred arrow" into the ground
and tethering themselves to it with a rawhide or
a leather thong. They would await their enemy in
that place, vowing to leave only when the enemy
was defeated or death took its toll. There was no
retreat from the stake. The enemy almost never
gave quarter. Oftentimes enemies took their time

and great pleasure in surrounding a staked-out Dog Soldier and killing him a cut and a slice at a time. A Dog Soldier was held in high esteem by all concerned, be they friend or enemy.

Jared fell to his face in uncontrollable weakness, overwhelmed by the words that had just pierced his heart. The power of this encounter was beyond description. He knew he had to make a decision now. He thought of his past, his brokenness and his sins. His decision was made within his heart for he knew that he had nothing of value within himself.

"I choose to follow YOU!"

The bolt of lightning and the resounding thunderclap seemed to come from nowhere and everywhere. It struck Jared with all the power of the universe and drove him to the ground. He lay there lifeless, not breathing, heart not beating. He had no consciousness, no life. He was dead.

All the birds, animals, insects, spirits, all of life stood in awe at the power of I AM. There was complete silence. Nothing moved. All was still. Even the air was motionless.

The Great Bear, the Messenger Eagle, and the Sacrificial Man all stood and witnessed that Jared was truly without life, without breath, without heartbeat. He was, in fact, dead. They bore witness to his death.

Then, with great care, the Warrior moved toward Jared's dead body, reached down and touched his remains. As He did so, the Messenger Eagle spread His mighty wings, causing the wind to stir; and the Great Bear blew His breath toward Jared's body. There followed a great eruptive explosion! Greater and brighter lightning than before, in unison with a greater thunderclap than before, struck Jared's body! The ground quaked, then shook as his body spasmed as though electrified, then slowly rose, standing upright with a brightness and power about him that had never been there before. He stood up, one who had been dead but was now alive! He stood before his Creator, took in a deep breath, and laughed with great joy! He was full of new life! His eyes shone as though on fire. His body glowed with the intensity of the noonday sun.

The birds and animals that had fallen silent suddenly erupted into joyous singing. Music came from the trees, the leaves, the clouds, from everywhere! The very stones cried out! Human voices and angelic voices joined in, singing and shouting with laughter. The wind made a sound that was more than sound but became movement, changing the very atmospheric pressure. Musical instruments joined into the celebrative mixture, chorusing into a symphony of joy! Great horns and stringed instruments of all kinds joined in. Drumbeats came from everywhere, accompanied by heart sound vocables from the ancient elders— "Hey ya hey ya hey ya! Yaweh!"

Jared wept like a child as his heart was healed of the deep wounds that had crippled him spiritually and emotionally his whole life. His life passed before him, the pain-filled moments, the sins against him, the deep wounds within, and they were escorted from his life by the Power-That-Is-Greater-Than-All. He was cleansed by the mighty but gentle hand of He-Who-Heals-From-Within. Then, the wrongs that he had committed against others, the "coyote" times, the stealing, the lying, the deceiving, the sexual sins, the hatred sins, the anger sins, all were poured out before him. They lifted from him as though they had never been there. He felt the Creator's breath fill his lungs, then his heart and mind and soul. He was permeated by the combined breath of the Great Bear, the Warrior, and the Giant Eagle with its wings of spirit wind. He felt himself filled with life and power. He felt his spirit awakening.

"I have been so wrong, so wrong. I'm so sorry, Grandfather." He wept and confessed his darkness before the Creator, His Warrior Son, and His Spirit Messenger. It was a powerful time of cleansing and awakening for Jared Spotted-Horse, for he was quite literally in the presence of Creator of Heaven and earth.

Jared came to understand things that he had been unable to fathom before. His spirit began to reconnect with He-Who-Had-Given-It. He began to understand. He was able to forgive, to let go of the pain and the fear. He was set free. He was a new creation! Given new life! The old Jared was dead, killed by Creator. Then he was re-created and given new life with a new nature of love. The new Jared stood before Creator.

The Great Bear looked at him.

"Jared, remember these words and take them back to your people:

"You have been kept as a remnant people to be awakened before the end of days. It is time to awake, O people of the River. Awake and return to your Creator who loves you and calls you. Awake and return so that others may return with you. I will restore to you things that have been lost through the disobedience of those who are 'called by my name.' I will teach you how to heal the land. I will show you the truth of who I AM. You will all dance again. You will all drum again. You will possess the land again. Come to the River of Life; Come to the Ancient of Days. Come to Grandfather. Honor My Son; and My Great Spirit will honor you!'"

The Great Warrior spoke.

"Jared Spotted-Horse, I give you another name. Some will choose to know you as Jared Spotted-Horse. I will call you 'Walks in Spirit.' Share this name with others if it pleases you, or not, but I will always address you by this name." He smiled as He turned.

Jared watched as the Warrior, the Great Bear, and the Messenger Eagle turned and departed up the trail. He watched as the animals trailed in behind them, forming an honor guard. He stared in amazement as the whirling birds and insects worshipped while flittering, swooping, and diving above and around and behind the three Great Ones.

Then he saw a familiar figure standing, watching him, smiling. Jack. That ex-hippy-turned-logger, that hillside preacher, the friend who would give him the shirt off his back. He smiled, waved, and moved toward the others. Jared waved back, calling out, "Goodbye, Jack! I love you!"

Jared spied someone he hadn't noticed before. It was Aunt Mary, a very young and beautiful Aunt Mary, a glowing Aunt Mary. She was walking with two small boys. They were smiling and squealing with joy, waving their little arms and jumping up and down.

"Tell Ree I love him and miss him. Tell him Chetco and Shasta are with me and we're happy and waiting for him." She smiled a most loving and radiant smile.

"Tell Daddy, tell Daddy we love him. Tell him to hurry!" The boys hollered in unison as they moved along with the departing caravan, their little voices echoing in the standing timber.

Jared collapsed again, trembling and weeping, unable to control himself or to see through his blurred eyes. The Great Bear, the Messenger Eagle, and the Warrior were almost out of sight when the Warrior stopped, turned, smiled, and pointed. Jared followed the gesture, looking to a small grassy hill, and spotted a familiar form, a beautiful young lady's form. He couldn't, he dare not believe, who and what he was seeing. The young tribal lady, with braided black glistening hair and dressed in a long, white, beaded and fringed buckskin dress, turned and looked at him. She smiled the biggest smile he had ever seen. She was alive, here! Mom! She opened both arms to him, as though inviting him to run into them as he had as a little boy. She held the pose, then with one hand, threw him a kiss, which he caught and touched to his own tear-drenched, quivering lips.

He glanced at the Warrior, who nodded and smiled and whispered these words: "She called on My Name with her last breath, and I heard her! And We brought her Home."

She nodded at her son, blew another kiss, raised her outstretched arms into a posture of praise and thanks, then turned. With head held high she pulled the white dance shawl over her shoulders and, walking as a traditional tribal woman walks, with great dignity, she rejoined the Grand Entry back into Creator's Heaven. She turned for just a moment and spoke: "I love you, Walks in Spirit. I always did. I always will. Until your time comes, walk strong and walk gently. Serve the people with your vision; and serve Him." She gestured toward the Great Warrior, turned, and was gone.

Jared's mother followed the Warrior as He turned to go. Behind her Jared saw his aunties, uncles, cousins, grandparents, young, strong and happy. He saw friends. He saw Jimmy-the-Fox, laughing and waving. Jimmy had called out to Yeshua as he had lain there in the snow, bleeding. He had reached out a hand with the last of his strength toward the Heavens and had spoken the name... Jesus. Truly the Creator had been merciful.

Jared asked the Warrior, "Tell me, please: what is your name?"

"I AM Yeshua. I AM the Lion of my Tribe. I commission you a warrior and a servant; serve me and serve your people. Remember this: you will never walk alone again."

With that, He turned and rejoined the Grand Entry. The drum resounded when the Warrior returned to His rightful place of honor at the head of the procession. His voice rose as He joined in the singing and dancing. His regalia swayed with the beat of the drum and the steps of His moccasin-clad feet.

The birds and music faded into silence as Creator and company departed. A strong wind came up and blew through the trees, causing them to bend in honor of the Great One's passing. The moon sent rays through the standing timber, shedding soft light upon the departing Deity. Jared raised his hand, then bowed his head and finally allowed the tears of joy and mourning and grieving to flow freely and with abandon. He collapsed onto his blanket, barely able to breathe; he didn't want to return to the physical world. He wanted to rise up and follow the Great One into His Heaven, but he didn't have the strength. He lay on the blanket—weak, trembling, and smiling. He slept.

32

Walks in Spirit

He had not wanted to come back. Shad had helped him, giving him water, walking with him down the trail, holding him up, keeping him moving. Jared staggered and fell several times but Shad helped break his falls. He was in and out of consciousness, crossing back and forth between the two worlds. He was broken in every way and was confused and emotional on the trip back to camp. Finally, upon their return, he slept again.

He awoke to the smell of trout and eggs. He was back in camp at Shasta Costa Creek, Old Tecumtum's camp. How he had gotten here he didn't know. He stepped out of the tent into dazzling sunlight and took a deep breath, taking in the smells of the camp and the forest. Shad was bent over the fire turning the fish. He looked up with a smile and a wink. "I would say you had yourself a vision, from the look on your face."

Jared was in wonder over what he had seen. His body felt weak and used up. He told Shad he wasn't ready to talk about it yet, but yes, he had seen, had experienced something powerful. His good wolf was in charge.

They ate by the quiet of the creek, interrupted from time to time by a blue jay or a magpie. The riffle had a language of its own as water cascaded over boulders and took rest in swirling eddies. A mayfly touched the glistening surface just in time to become a meal for a tenacious rainbow trout, reminding Jared that he was now back in the physical world. As they ate their breakfast in contemplation, chewing slowly, they witnessed the cycle of life unfolding before them and wondered at the delicate and balanced order of it all. And of course they admired the handiwork of Creator Himself.

Not much was said as they rested over the next couple of days. Shad was considering his next assignment and was clearly in a fasting and praying mode. Jared was sorting things out as best he could while regaining his physical strength. After having seen his Vision he was anxious to get back to someone who would understand it and help him to live it out. Of course that someone was Sherri.

He had a deep feeling that she would understand the significance of the Sacrificial Warrior Who had "given" Himself for the people, the Great Bear Who dared not allow Jared to see His "fullness," and the majestic Eagle Messenger. He had much to think about and even more to understand.

He was also the bearer of a powerful message for his tribal people. But he didn't really understand all that either. What did "end of days" mean, anyway?

He knew beyond a shadow of a doubt that Sherri was the girl for him. He would tell her all of his history, every bit of it. He didn't want anything to come from his past to waylay their relationship.

He rested for three more days at Old John's Camp. He came to understand Shad as one of those unusual fellows who lives for Creator and follows the lead of The Great Messenger Eagle. They exchanged few words, as is the tribal way. They spent time together, fished, and rested by the fire in the evenings. They enjoyed fine coffee and solitude. Shad was a traveler who would move on within a day or two in order to reach a destination not of his own choosing, but who was willing and happy nonetheless.

Jared considered the possibility that Shad was

an angel but discarded that as unlikely. He finally concluded that he was a servant on the earth. Whatever he was, Jared was thankful for him and told him so.

He shook hands with Shad, knowing that he would never see him again this side of eternity, then fired up his Ford and headed downstream. He didn't know what lay ahead but he knew he was not the same man he had been a few days ago. He also knew that he couldn't accomplish whatever it was he was meant to accomplish without the help of a certain little gal with hazel and green eyes.

"Good-bye and Godspeed, Walks in Spirit." Shad prayed as he watched him drive away.

Jared prayed: "Please, Lord, Creator, help me to be honorable and good to this woman. I know you have given me a message to deliver with this new life. Help me to find my way."

As he turned north onto the Coast Highway, he believed that Sherri would fill in the blanks concerning what he had seen and how to approach his new life. He felt as though he had been born all over again. And he wanted to know where to get the Book of Heaven the Warrior had referred to. As he crossed the big river—Tolhut Tahilee—a giant Eagle soared across the expanse of pale cobalt sky in front of him, dipped a wing, and flew on. He smiled in recognition.

He looked down and spotted the little gift sack that Sherri had given him. He hadn't gotten around to opening it. As he did, steering with his left hand and opening the paper sack with his right, he saw the sticky-note stuck to the little green Gideon New Testament: "Just a little gift. I recently heard this referred to as 'THE BOOK OF HEAVEN.' Enjoy, my love, S."

About the author

Dan Lundy lives on the Oregon coast with his wife, LaRita, and their dog, Joy Bells. They own a consulting firm that provides project management services to logging and construction companies. Dan was educated at Northwest Christian University (bachelors) and Colorado Technical University (masters).

Dan and LaRita are the founding pastors of Sacred Ground Outreach Church in Siletz, Oregon. They are presently involved in a boat ministry, skippering the M/V *Messenger* together as they reach out to Native Americans in the remote coastal villages of Alaska. They cherish spending time with their children, grandchildren, and great-grandchildren.

Dan loves to drift the Siletz River and fish for salmon and steelhead. He also enjoys fly fishing for cutthroat trout and elk hunting.

Dan is a Siletz tribal elder. He writes songs and poems. *Vision Quest* is his first novel.

CPSIA information can be obtained
at www.ICGtesting.com
Printed in the USA
FSOW01n2029211014
3273FS